RAVINE

RAVINE

by *Janet Hickman*

GREENWILLOW BOOKS
An Imprint of HarperCollins*Publishers*

Ravine

Copyright © 2002 by Janet Hickman

All rights reserved. No part of this book may be
used or reproduced in any manner whatsoever without
written permission except in the case of brief
quotations embodied in critical articles and reviews.
Printed in the United States of America.
For information address HarperCollins Children's Books,
a division of HarperCollins Publishers,
1350 Avenue of the Americas, New York, NY 10019.
www.harperchildrens.com

The text of this book is set in Meridian.

Library of Congress Cataloging-in-Publication Data

Hickman, Janet.
Ravine / by Janet Hickman.
p.   cm.
"Greenwillow Books."
Summary: As Ulf searches for a friend to ease his difficult life
in the castle keep of a cruel king and queen and, in a very
different time and place, Jeremy looks for adventure in
the war games he plays with his best friend, the two
boys are brought together by Jeremy's dog.
ISBN 0-688-17952-5 (trade).   ISBN 0-06-029367-5 (lib. bdg.)
[1. Space and time—Fiction.]   I. Title.
PZ7.H5314 Rav 2002   [Fic]—dc21   2001042493

1   2   3   4   5   6   7   8   9   10   First Edition

FOR ALEX

CHAPTER 1

❖ *Ulf*

They called him the wizard's boy, but his real name was
Ulf, and he was lonely. In all the time he had lived among
these people, no boy had befriended him. Everyone knew
he was an outlander, a child taken during a raid on his
mother's faraway village and carried back to serve the
royal household of Ludwig and his queen. Ulf had spent
his days as ordered, season after season, fetching water in
jars he could scarcely lift and dodging blows for slowness
and spillage.

None showed the boy any kindness in that household
except for the young woman called Gudrun the Fair. She
had chambers of her own in the queen's corridor, but often
she came like a servant to carry water as Ulf did. She

smiled when she spoke to him, and even such a small thing soothed the loneliness inside him. But she carried more grief than water, that was plain to him. Once when they rested, she touched his thatch of sun-colored hair and said, "Poor boy. Your story is as pitiful as my own." But he did not ask her to explain, for he was always tongue-tied in her presence.

At the end of each day, when the most-favored servants went off to their sleeping mats in the great house, the cook gave Ulf a heel of bread or a bit of meat—it never seemed enough—and sent him out with the other luckless ones who slept in the stables. Ulf went his own way then, and none of the others ever quite dared to call him back, for they knew well enough where he went. Long before, during a time of ice, the wizard Harket and his wife, Old Berta, had come upon Ulf outside the queen's stables. He was struggling toward the warmth inside while bigger lads barred his way and laughed and pushed him, claiming the shelter for themselves. The old couple had led him off, without a word, to their hut below the forest at the stream's edge. They gave him soup and a length of wool and a corner for sleeping, that night and thereafter. At first he was wary of the strangeness about them, but he grew accustomed to their soft singing and the fragrance of herbs that hung always in the air. He soon learned to take no offense when in daytime the other servants muttered and called him "wizard's boy" behind their hands. He thought it was not such a bad thing to be. But the wizard and his wife were given to silence, and so, both day and night, Ulf was lonely.

And then, one evening on his way to the wizard's hut, he met unexpected company. The air was chill, and fog swirled up from the river to hide his feet as he walked through the deep cut of the stream at the forest's end. He glanced up toward the high path that led along the rocky bank, where the air was still clear, and saw an animal come bounding over the track and partway down the steep slope. At first Ulf mistook it for a deer, but when it stopped, he squinted through the gray twilight and saw that it must be a dog. Even so, it looked nothing like the queen's hounds or the curs that hung about the kitchen. This was a dog such as he had never seen before. It had long, shimmering hair the color of summer honey and a great plume of a tail. When it stopped, it held itself motionless as a carving in the king's table. Watching, Ulf began to think how big it was, how near his own size, and he wondered if he should fear it.

Then the dog moved its long muzzle, fastened its gaze on Ulf, and began to swing its tail. A low whistle rose to the boy's lips. He had not planned to whistle, but the sound came out of him as naturally as breathing. For a moment nothing happened. Then the dog came scrambling down into the mist and sat at his feet.

Ulf held his breath, not quite believing what he saw. It

must be a miracle, he thought, for he wanted a dog, a companion such as this. He had not dreamed of one so fine, but still—

"Good dog," he whispered, and when he stepped closer, he could tell it was a female. He stroked her head with a cautious hand, and she leaned happily against his leg.

Suddenly Ulf's delight turned to panic, for all at once, on the high path from which the dog had come, there sounded a crashing of drums and a wailing of voices. He flung himself down, urging the animal to follow him toward the shelter of a bush. At least the fog would be some protection, he thought, against the warrior horde that he expected to see come riding by on the heights. He waited there in the damp, trembling, but no troop appeared. There was only the terrible rhythm above and the dog's tail swishing beside him.

Finally Ulf rose to peer about him, but the mist moved upward and curled on itself with such speed that he was not sure of his eyes. He thought he saw three figures on the path, three strangers—two of them a bit taller than himself and the other quite small. The little one carried a box with shiny bits on the side and what Ulf knew to be a mighty enchantment, for all the sound of drumming and screeching was trapped inside it and pouring out. The two bigger ones called back and forth in loud voices—Ulf had never seen such disrespect for danger—but they might have been geese in Old Berta's pen for all he understood their words. Much as he tried to hold his courage, a shudder went through him. Just then the terrible music ceased and all three of the figures on the hillside began to whistle and call in a shrill chorus that echoed up and down the ravine. Immediately the dog slid out of Ulf's grasp and trotted up the bank, out of sight.

"Come back!" Ulf cried as loud as he dared, but look as he might, he could not see the dog's shape above him, nor could he make out the others. He stood alone, trying to hear beyond the ripple of the stream, to see beyond the fog. He began to think his eyes and ears had played tricks on him, that he had been awake and dreaming. There was no sign now of anyone on the high path.

But the dog had been no dream. "Dog!" he called softly. "Come back!" Ulf put out of his mind whatever unknown dangers might be feared from three boy-sized creatures disappearing in the fog. He made the sign to ward off evil, and then he began to think about the dog—his dog, maybe, if he could find her again.

Harket and Old Berta seldom asked for conversation, or offered it, but Ulf was too full of thoughts and hopes that night to be quiet. "There was fog in the ravine," he told them, "and when I walked along the stream, a splendid dog came down over the rocks to me." The wizard's wife smiled and scraped out the stew pot to feed the boy.

"Its fur hung down over its legs, like a woman's skirt," he said. Old Berta shook her head in disbelief.

"Around her neck and on the feet it was pure white," he continued, "and . . . and . . ." He struggled to remember each detail of its beauty. "Her eyes were not dark like the eyes of a dog, but gray as a winter sky."

Harket frowned, and Old Berta's hands went still. "Was it a wolf, then?" she said.

"No! It was no wolf," insisted Ulf with his mouth full.

Breaking silence, Harket leaned across the rough table so far that Ulf could see, one by one, the hairs of the wizard's white beard. "What else did you see?" the old man asked softly.

Ulf looked at his food. "The fog swirled," he said. "I would not have seen the dog if it had not come to me."

"Look at me, boy." Harket's voice was so solemn that Ulf's heart pounded. He had never been afraid in the wizard's hut, had never seen illusions there, nor any display of power. All he knew of wizardry was the sound of chanting and the countless odors of smoke. Yet now there was a tightness in the air and a force he could not name that seemed to pull his chin up. He could not have looked away from Harket even if he had been brave enough to try.

"Did you speak to that animal?" Soft as it was, the wizard's voice filled up the little room.

"I did," whispered Ulf.

"Did you touch it?"

"I touched it."

Ulf heard Berta draw in her breath, a little sound of alarm.

Harket brought his face so close to Ulf's that the boy began to shake and could not stop. "I tell you this now, boy, though it may be too late. If that dog comes again, hide yourself. Do not speak to it. Do not call it. Above all, do not touch it."

Every word was slow and clear and terrible to Ulf's ears, but the wizard's eyes no longer held his, and so he bent his head.

"I am sorry, Harket," he mumbled after a moment. He had too much fright in him now to think of telling the parts he had left out of his tale.

The old man rose slowly from his bench. "The consequences are beyond your imagining, boy," he said, but he rested one hand kindly on Ulf's shoulder as he spoke. The wizard beckoned his wife, and the two of them went to sit behind the corner curtain, which hid a gleaming pot of coals and jar after jar of roots and dry leaves and precious powders—Ulf had looked at all of it once when he was by himself in the hut and had decided it was better left alone. Soon he could hear the beginning of their singing, no louder than the drone of two insects on a summer night, and soon his nose was full of an irresistible scent.

And then Ulf lay down, thinking he could not ever sleep again, but of course he did.

❖ *Jeremy*

Jeremy hadn't expected to see fog come creeping up out of the ravine, swirling low along Morning Street. In the twilight it seemed to separate the old houses from their foundations and the trees from their roots.

Perfect, Jeremy thought. Like magic. You could hide an army down there in fog like that. Well, a whole bunch of guys anyway. And then they would come crashing up over the edge and it would be so weird because it would look like they didn't have any legs. The other guys who were just marching along totally minding their own business would be totally freaked out, and they'd break ranks and run, and—

"Hey, Quinn!" he called to the boy who walked ahead of him. "You know what we could do with our game board, maybe? We could make the edge of it like a ravine and then we could have like a little fog machine, and then . . ." He paused for breath, thinking of the huge plywood battlefield that rested more or less safely on four overturned wastebaskets in Quinn's basement. It was cluttered with ancient warriors, tiny ones, smaller than his thumb: Quinn's troops and his own.

"And what?" Quinn said, turning enough for Jeremy to see that he had already finished the little bag of chips from their stop at the convenience store. Quinn was half a year older than Jeremy, a lot taller, a better ballplayer, one grade ahead in school. He was commander in chief to Jeremy's subordinate general, noble knight to Jeremy's simple soldier, every time. Not that Jeremy minded. He and Quinn were best friends. They kept each other company in a neighborhood where people their age were scarce.

"*You* know what fog would be good for," Jeremy said. "Surprise attacks and stuff. Besides, it would look so cool."

"And where do we get this little fog machine?"

Jeremy shrugged. "You might know how to make one, I thought."

A grin spread across the other boy's face. "Yeah, right. Me and Einstein."

Jeremy shrugged again. "I just thought, maybe . . ." he said. He kicked through the soggy leaves along the side of the street, hating to let go of the idea of fog curling onto their battlefield and swallowing up their model soldiers. He squinted his eyes, trying to imagine the scene as real, right here along Morning Street, but the effect was ruined by the wrong background music—the din of his little brother's boom box up ahead and just out of sight. Ancient warriors meet hip-hop. Disgusting.

"Austin!" he shouted. "Turn that thing down!" For whole long stretches of the afternoon, he had been able to ignore Austin so completely that he had almost forgotten his little brother was with them. Why did he have to have a four-year-old tagging along when he was with Quinn? Why did his mother have to be so deep in her writing on a Saturday that she couldn't watch Austin herself? And why did Richelle have to be at the mall the entire day, for pete's sake? Richelle was Quinn's older sister and the one who usually watched Austin when Jeremy's mother was busy.

The radio's music was still thumping at high volume when Jeremy and Quinn rounded the curve by the dead oak tree and saw that Austin was crying.

"What's the matter?" Quinn said, but Jeremy didn't have to ask. He saw the leash and empty collar in Austin's hand, and his heart sank.

"Where's Duchess?" he said. "What happened to her?" He had told Austin not to bring the dog. It was hard to hold her when she was excited, even without a radio to carry.

"She runned away!" Austin said, wiping the end of his jacket sleeve across his wet face. "She's a bad dog!" He began to tug at a lock of his own coppery hair. Jeremy knew what that sign meant—*in distress, wants comfort*—because Austin had been doing it since he was a baby. Jeremy felt sorry for him, but he was too upset himself to offer much sympathy. His mind was busy making pictures of Duchess, his beautiful dog, part collie, part mystery dog, in terrible trouble. *Chunk-a-thunk, woo,* went the radio, *chunk-a-thunk, thunk!*

"Don't cry," Jeremy managed to say, and then, "How long has she been gone? Which way did she go?"

Austin's face crumpled. "Down there!" he wailed, pointing into the ravine.

"Hey, yeah?" Quinn began to sound interested. "Let's go look for her. It would be a shortcut anyway. We just go down the bank here, across the stream and that little street, and up at an angle on the other side. It's only a block to your house."

Jeremy knew well enough where he was and how to get home, but he also knew what his mother would say. So did Quinn.

"You know I'm not supposed to be in the ravine," Jeremy said, and he could feel his forehead pinching up into the little worry lines that people at school teased him about. He took a breath. "But we can't just let Duchess be lost, either."

"So come on." Quinn walked to the edge and peered down. Jeremy followed. The light was murky, full of shapes that Jeremy couldn't recognize, even though he had studied the pattern of rocks and fallen limbs on this steep hillside many times in sunlight.

He shook his head. "Why don't we just try calling her first?"

"Because it would be more fun to go down there," said Quinn.

Jeremy sighed. He didn't want Quinn to think he was afraid. He hated that. Quinn never seemed to be afraid. But Jeremy knew what was sensible and what wasn't. People were always saying that about him. "Jeremy is a sensible boy," his teachers would write on his report card.

"Climbing down there can be plan B," Jeremy said. "Plan A is, we call her." He went back to where Austin was standing and clicked off the *chunk-a-thunk* music. Then he took a deep breath and whistled for Duchess. Austin helped, calling her name because he wasn't much of a whistler yet, and finally Quinn put two fingers in his mouth and split the air. When the sound faded, they did it all over again, and again. In a moment or two, the dog's head came rising out of the mist. Her front paws scrabbled the lip of the bank in front of them, and then there she stood, breathing hard.

Austin screeched, first for fright at the dog's ghostly way of appearing and next just for the pleasure of seeing her. "Good dog," he said. "Good Duchess. You came back."

Jeremy felt so much relief that he could have made plenty of noise on his own, but he settled for a few quick pats on the dog's head as he maneuvered her collar back in place. "Where have you been?" he whispered, winding the end of the leash an extra turn around his hand.

"We could still take the shortcut," Quinn said. "I could

get us down from here real easy. And now that Duchess has been down this way once, she could help, too."

"No." Jeremy sighed. "See how dark it is? We're late already and it wouldn't be any shortcut if someone fell in the dark." He paused. "Anyway, Austin might get hurt."

Quinn laughed. "Austin's like a little mountain goat," he said, which made Austin smile. "You're the one that's worried about falling, Jeremy."

"I am not!" The trouble was, Quinn might be right. Probably Quinn could find a path, even in the dark, and he, Jeremy, might stumble. Jeremy's father said that Quinn was a natural athlete. Quinn could do almost anything, Jeremy thought, with the possible exception of making a fog machine.

"Come on," he said to Austin. "We have to really hurry." Sometimes he wished that he and Quinn could trade families so Quinn could have the mother who worried and watched the clock and he could have the dad who wasn't home to see the clock and wouldn't have cared all that much anyway. But that wasn't how things were, and the streetlights were already coming on, and so they ran, with Quinn leading the way.

They trotted the whole length of Morning Street, turned on Sycamore Heights, and followed the sidewalk along the bridge over the ravine. They had to stop at the middle-school ball field to let Austin rest his legs, and finally Quinn took him pickaback. By the time they had followed the winding street to Jeremy's house and its brightly lit front porch, they were giddy with exertion, laughing at nothing. Duchess barked like a wild thing.

"Where have you boys been?" Jeremy's mother called the minute they set foot on the steps. "It's pitch dark. Is Austin all right?" She stood looking at them through the open window in her study, clutching a battered book like a shield across her chest. Automatically, Jeremy's eyes scanned the title: *Princess Legends from Northern Lands.* Boring, he thought. There were always stacks of books around the house when his mother was working on a big project, and once in a while they were interesting. Just yesterday he had found one with pictures of weapons from ancient times.

"Hi, Mommy!" Austin was shouting. "We're okay! Duchess runned away and made us late!"

Austin's explanation seemed to satisfy Jeremy's mother until Quinn had gone home and supper was over. After that, when Austin was tucked in bed with Duchess guarding his feet the way she always did before she went to Jeremy's room, the questions began. Jeremy knew that his mother wanted a complete geography of their afternoon. He tried to avoid the word she didn't want to hear, but she picked it up without his even saying it.

"Now, one more time, Jeremy," she said, "about the ravine. I know what a fascinating place it is, with the stream and the rocks and that little road that looks like it isn't going anywhere. I know how much you and Quinn would like to play in the ravine. But *stay away* from it. Understand?"

"Why?" said Jeremy. He and his mother had been through this talk so many times that it was as if there were a script for it, and this was his line, the one little word that he couldn't help saying, even though he knew it would keep his mother going on and on.

"The ravine has a reputation, Jeremy. Tough kids hang out down there. Not just neighborhood kids—they can drive in from anywhere. It's no place for you and certainly no place for Austin. Or Quinn, either, for that matter. I've heard two or three stories that just curled my hair." Jeremy smiled because his mother's hair was as straight as ever, brown and shiny and flat like his own.

"No one really knows what all happens," she went on, "but some of it's sure to be trouble, and I don't want you in trouble. So stay out of the ravine. It's as simple as that."

"*Annh,*" said Jeremy. It was a sound he had learned from his father, a sound that could mean either yes or no. "Can I go brush my teeth now?" he asked, because he had discovered it was a question that held just a little magic. Parents almost always quit bothering you when brushing was involved.

"Fine," said his mother, raising her hands palms-up in a

gesture of dismissal. "Brush away. But remember, no ravine."

"No ravine," Jeremy repeated without conviction. He thought about it while he brushed his teeth. With Duchess around, and Quinn, he didn't see how that could possibly work.

❖ *Ulf*

For days Ulf thought of the dog as he trudged from the wizard's hut to the royal house before sunrise and back again in the falling dark. He imagined her at his side as he dragged the heavy water jars into the stream each day. In his mind, he could see her lower her head, drink, and then walk beside him to the scullery door. Even the cook would see her and be astonished by her beauty. Much as he longed for the dog to appear, he dreaded it, too; for he did not know if he could stop his hands from touching her or his tongue from whispering an admiring word. Yet how would he dare to ignore Harket's warning? Once, very early in the day, he heard barking, but the sound did not come from the place where he had seen the dog and so he made his heart be still.

On that very same morning, King Ludwig and his war troop rode home from their journeying. For a while the uproar of the king's arrival drove every bit of wondering and worrying out of Ulf's head. There was no end to the basins and cooking pots that had to be filled, no rest from the new demands to fetch that and carry this and *thwack!* "Get out of the way, boy!" Ludwig strode around the compound and through his house, shouting orders as servants disappeared into corners and slipped like shadows behind the hanging tapestries. Ulf thought the king had not changed one little bit since his last time at home.

The royal son, Armut, was another matter. He had grown taller, and his beard had thickened. Men from the troop approached him with respect, although among themselves they called him Prince Ar, fondly, as if he were still a boy. Queen Erlinda swooped down on him the moment he dismounted his horse. Ulf saw it and felt no surprise, for everyone knew how strong a favorite was Prince Ar in the queen's eyes, how she doted on him and plotted punishment for anyone who dared to speak against him.

"Her Highness is fierce as a she-wolf," Harket had whispered once to Ulf. "Better if her glance never falls on you." It was habit now for Ulf to use every way he knew to be out of sight of all their majesties, even Princess Orrun, who was gentle as a meadow mouse.

So it was that Ulf trembled when Erlinda herself came to

the cook on the day of Ludwig's return to point out the boys who were to carry food to the king's table at his welcome feast. Ulf tried to make himself small as the queen's glance flicked around the room from one face to the next. At last she spoke some names and, as if it were an afterthought, looked again at Ulf.

"And this outlander," she said, speaking to the cook, "send him, too, to wait on the girl." Her lips curled around the last word. Ulf's knees began to wobble under him.

"Stand still, boy, and listen!" The queen took a step toward him. Light from the doorway fell on her face so that Ulf could see plainly how elegant her features were, and how unforgiving.

"You are to be silent as a stone behind our table," she said. "You will do as you are bid and say no word about it, then or after—or I will have you thrashed, and worse." Her dark eyes glittered. "Do you know what I have said?"

"Yes, majesty," Ulf mumbled, not daring to ask who it was that he had been chosen to wait upon. Dread settled behind his eyes and grew inside him all that day, and then finally the feasting torches were lit and the jars he carried were filled with mead instead of water.

He had not served at dinner in the great hall before, and he was wary of the noise of it and the leaping shadows and the press of people—officers of the troop and handmaids and royal kinsmen who usually kept to their own quarters. The day had been long already, and Ulf's body ached. What if his hands turned clumsy? What if he forgot to lower his eyes as a sign of respect if the king should look at him?

"Ulf! There!" The cook found him at the doorway and pointed, starting him off with a shove that was none too gentle. "Stand behind, and be ready to hop fast as a flea."

Ulf nodded, and as he moved slowly toward his place, he noted how the family had arranged themselves at the royal table that night. First was Orrun, the princess, and then the king himself. At his side was the queen, and there at her elbow the favored Prince Ar. Finally, on the prince's left and at the far corner of the table, sat the girl Ulf was to serve. She was as pale as she was beautiful, gowned in finery like the others, but showing no hint of pleasure in the midst of all their merriment. Ulf blinked as he drew nearer, thinking the firelight had tricked him, but he could not mistake the glint of her hair. It was Gudrun, the girl who carried water.

Serving her was no work at all, Ulf discovered, for she ate nothing, drank nothing. She never once raised her head, not even when Prince Ar leaned close and spoke with a smile against the curls that covered her ear. It was only Ulf's great curiosity about Gudrun's place at the table that kept him from falling asleep and into disaster. The glow of the great hearth that warmed the backs of the royal family heated him near to sizzling and made his eyelids droop.

Once, when Prince Ar's own serving boy was busy, the

prince summoned Ulf to fill his goblet. Ar had turned to speak to the queen by then, and Ulf could not avoid hearing.

". . . have taken poor care of her," the prince said. His tone was low and insistent. "I see how thin she is, and how she has the hands of a scullery maid. How will she ever agree to it if she is treated ill?"

Ulf caught his breath and stepped back as the queen said a few sharp words that made the prince scowl and turn away. After a moment Ulf saw him speak again to Gudrun, but the girl shook her head, and there were more whispers and fierce looks between mother and son. Finally, the prince rose up out of his seat and strode away from the table and out of the great hall, spreading silence after him.

Ludwig stood then, commanding the attention of his subjects and directing them to continue their feast. He offered his regret that the royal family had decided to seek rest instead of revelry. One of his hands he held out to the queen, the other to his daughter, and together all three of them swept out of the hall. At the doorway, Orrun turned a sad face back over her shoulder toward the place where Gudrun still sat.

One of the other serving boys gave Ulf a poke in the ribs. "Close up your mouth, gawker," he said. "It's nothing to do with you. And see to your end of the table!"

Ulf gave himself a shake and began to gather empty platters. He did not know what to do about the silent young woman who sat alone. He liked her. She had been kind to him. "Will you eat now?" he asked at last. "Or am I to take it away?" Wanting a smile from her, he tried a small one of his own.

She pushed her things toward him. "I am glad it is you," she said, in a voice that was thin and tight. "You remind me of home, of my brother when we both were small. But he is grown now, and he will come for me." Then she did look up at Ulf with just the shadow of a smile. "You should find a good, safe hiding place," she whispered. "I am a princess in my own land, and when my people come for me, there will be great shedding of blood."

Ulf frowned and nodded, although he was not sure he understood. The part that was clear to him was Gudrun's distress, and it filled him with a great, impossible desire to comfort her. Instead he escaped to the kitchen with his stack of platters. There he kept busy until the cook, in a fit of good temper, told him to help himself to the scraps and go off to bed.

It seemed to Ulf already like the dead of night. His feet found their own way down to the stream and along it without any help from his head. He had taken a huge bone as his portion for the night, one with rich bits of roast meat clinging to it still, one big enough that Berta might have used it for a week of soup. But it began to seem too heavy and too slippery to carry, and finally he put his arm over his head and threw the bone as far up the bank as his strength would allow.

"Come get it, dog," he mumbled. Moments later, when the effort to keep awake made him stumble and sway, a strong old arm circled his shoulders, and the wizard led him home.

❊ *Jeremy*

As far as Jeremy was concerned, that Friday started as a perfect day. There was no school for kids, but a whole long schedule of meetings for teachers. It was such a simple but satisfying arrangement; he hoped the school would announce another day like it very soon. Friday off meant Thursday was a free night, and he had spent it at Quinn's house, sleeping over—one of his favorite things. There was a big square of shaggy carpet in Quinn's basement where they spread their sleeping bags, an old television with a VCR for watching their favorite movies, and, for snacks, a dented mini-refrigerator that Quinn's dad had used in his college rooming house years and years ago. Mr. DaSilva never seemed in any hurry to get to the radio station where he worked; on this morning he had let Quinn and Jeremy sleep almost until lunchtime, wakening them with the aroma of frying bacon. Jeremy's stomach was full and his face was cheerful. The whole day stretched ahead with no school and no Austin. Richelle was baby-sitting. She had to get up early, Jeremy supposed, to have time to walk over to his house before his mother left for work. But he and Quinn had been kind to Richelle. They hadn't crept upstairs and taped her door shut during the night, the way they had first planned.

"Don't you guys forget to check in with Richelle," Mr. DaSilva said, as if he might have known that Jeremy was thinking about her.

"Yeah, sure," Quinn said. "We will." Jeremy thought they probably wouldn't. They almost never did. Everything would be fine unless Richelle brought Austin and came looking for them.

"I'll be late again, Quinn," Mr. DaSilva said as he put on his coat. "But listen, you boys ought to get out and do some things today. Don't stay down in the basement all the time. There's not all that much good weather left."

Jeremy frowned in the direction of Mr. DaSilva's back as the door closed after him. He had had such good luck on the battlefield the evening before, had captured so many of Quinn's warriors and so many miniature weapons, that he couldn't think of any other thing that would seem like fun to do.

"You know what?" he said to Quinn, who was bent over the comics section of the morning paper. "We could have an open-air battle today. We could take our guys outside and use stones and grass and moss and stuff, like the real thing."

Quinn looked up. "Okay," he said. "Sweet. But let's start over with our own guys again, and I get to pick the place."

Jeremy made a face. He didn't want to give up everything he had gained the night before, especially the archers. But taking the battle outside sounded so good that he decided not to argue. The fighting ground Quinn chose was at the very end of his street, where the pavement closed itself off in a semicircle. Beyond that, bushes and weeds and trees grew helter-skelter, and the ground fell away toward the ravine.

"Look over on the other side," Quinn said. "Way down to the right. That's where Duchess was that day, remember?"

Jeremy remembered and wished for his dog, but not too hard. She had been known to chew up entire armies of plastic warriors. He was more intent on finding the perfect rock, the best fallen limb, the super-most strategic position for his troops. He thought it was great the way the dust eddied up around them as he moved them from place to place—it was so realistic.

Jeremy turned his carrying case upside down and tapped the bottom to make sure every last warrior was out. Two skirmishers dropped onto the ground, and one piece of paper floated after them.

"What's this?" Quinn said, making a grab for it.

"You can look," Jeremy told him. "It's just some battle plans I drew."

"No. I mean on the other side, where the writing is."

Jeremy glanced at the page. "I took some of my mom's scrap paper," he said. "She starts with some other language at the top, and then she tries to get it to sound right in English down below. See?"

"Yeah," said Quinn. "Okay." He studied the paper so long that Jeremy began to drum his fingers on the empty case.

"Did you read it, Jeremy?"

Jeremy rolled his eyes upward. "If I took time to read every piece of paper my mother recycled, I'd have to drop out of school and give up sleeping."

Quinn laughed. "Listen to this, though." He cleared his throat. "*King*—Somebody, I can't pronounce it—*gathered his army and they followed after King Ludwig, who had stolen away his daughter. On an island far from shore*—old Somebody, the first guy—*found Ludwig, and the two kings locked themselves in a fight so bitter that one must die before the end of it.* We could set that battle up right here, Jeremy!"

"One-on-one's no fun," Jeremy said. His heart was set on the kind of battle they usually played.

"The first king had an army," Quinn argued, "and I'll bet Ludwig did, too, whoever he was."

Jeremy frowned. "It's probably wrong, somehow. My mom doesn't throw them away unless they're wrong."

"What's the difference?" Quinn said. "Come on. I'll be Ludwig, and you be the other guy, and that rock over there could be the island, and you put your army off to the left, and I'll put mine in front, and—" Quinn went on and on, and finally Jeremy agreed, just so they wouldn't waste any more time.

Quinn decided they should move to a rock formation that was just a little way down the bank, and so they dragged their supply boxes after them and drew new battle lines. Later on they saw a partly hollow log that was too good to pass up, and their fighting men faced off across a barrier of sickly gray fungus. There were so many fascinating places for trying out new troop arrangements that Quinn seemed to forget about the king with the unpronounceable name. Jeremy was glad. Even so, they didn't take time for a real battle, the kind that used dice to dictate the progress of the game. They just kept moving their men here and there and everywhere.

"Over here!"

"Wait! Look at this!"

"Come on!"

Back and forth it went, until Jeremy stood to stretch his legs.

"Quinn!" he said. "Look where we are." Much farther down the hillside than he had realized, that's where. He wouldn't have called it definitely *in* the ravine, but he was sure his mother would.

"Aw, Jeremy, relax." Quinn didn't even look up. "It's safe down in this part. I've been here before, lots of times. And if you don't pay attention, I'll move on your flank and take all the skirmishers you've got."

Jeremy leaned over and rescued his ancient warriors in one quick movement. "Let's pick up our stuff," he said, "before we lose some of it." They had left tiny guards posted all along their path, and now, looking back toward the top, he was certain some of them were already gone forever among the season's bright leaves.

Quinn shrugged. "Things were just getting good, I thought." He picked an acorn off the ground and tossed it down the hill. "Bet I can throw farther than you can," he said, reaching for more.

"I bet you can, too," Jeremy said, but he took the acorns Quinn handed him. Part of being Quinn's friend was joining in all the impromptu tests of skill that Quinn thought up. Jeremy always lost. *Zwishh!* went Quinn's first shot. Jeremy didn't even bother to throw. *Zwishh, zwishh, zwishh!*

"Take that, you evil enemy king!" Quinn bellowed as the acorns flew.

Jeremy laughed and got into the spirit of the event. "Quinn the Human Catapult!" he shouted, flinging his handful of ammunition as far as he could.

"Hey! Ow!" A voice came up from the winding street below, and then a person came into view, a large, high-school-type person who was rubbing his head and starting up the hillside toward them.

"Run, Quinn!" Jeremy whispered. "Come on!"

They turned and scrambled upward, going on a slant because it seemed easier, and crouching as they ran.

"You'd better run, you little oinkers!" the older boy shouted.

Jeremy and Quinn puffed along in silence, steadying themselves on low-hanging limbs, not daring to look back for fear of losing ground. Finally Jeremy had to stop to catch his breath, and that was when he realized their pursuer had given up on them. One minute Jeremy was as relieved as he had ever been in his life. The next minute, he took a step forward, and the ground gave way beneath his feet.

"Hey, Jeremy!" said Quinn. "That guy left! Jeremy— Where'd you go, Jeremy?" Quinn peered back into the alder thicket he had just passed. "Jeremy!"

"Here! Down here!" Jeremy's voice squeaked as he struggled to make himself heard. He had stumbled through the edge of the thicket into an enclosure of some kind, a little cave, a sunken hollow in the hillside. There was very little light and such a strong smell of damp earth that he sneezed and sputtered. "Quinn, come look!"

Just then his friend pulled back the right clump of bushes, and a shaft of afternoon light filled the place that Jeremy had found.

"It's like a foxhole or something," Jeremy said, taking advantage of the sudden brightness to gather up the model warriors that had spilled out of his hand when he fell.

"Nah." Quinn held the bushes back with his foot and twisted around for a better look. "It's too big for a foxhole," he said. "Maybe it's a fort."

Jeremy didn't think so, but he didn't want to disagree. He let his eyes rest on a little heap of flat stones at the rear of the enclosure and a length of tree trunk that would make a place to sit. "Who do you think built this place, Quinn?"

Quinn shrugged. "Who cares?" he said. "But who do you think could use it for secret battles, huh? It would be just as good as the hill, maybe better, and we'd have some protection from guys like Abominable Ravineman down there."

Jeremy smiled. He didn't understand what it was that made Quinn such a pure genius sometimes; this was just one more example of it. "Yeah," he said slowly, nodding his head to show Quinn how much he appreciated the idea. Even so, there was a warning tickle somewhere in his stomach. This was in the ravine, after all.

"Want to go get the stuff and start now?" Quinn bounced a little, showing how ready he was.

"What time is it?" Jeremy asked. "I don't want my mom to kill me for being late again."

"She wouldn't," Quinn said without telling him the time, so Jeremy knew it was late.

"We need to see if we can find all our warriors while there's still enough light," Jeremy said reasonably, and then they both sighed, because neither one of them liked the picking-up part of the game. There were so many places to look as the sun's rays stretched thinner that repacking their supply boxes took twice as long as usual. Quinn walked home with Jeremy—to protect Jeremy from his mother, Quinn said, and to avoid Richelle if he could.

On the way home, Jeremy thought that his mother would see how dirty he was and how late he was and do something terrible, like telling him he was grounded for the rest of the weekend. But when they came to Jeremy's house, his mother hardly gave him a look. She was just getting out of her car with an awkward armload of books and folders. Austin was pulling at her skirt and jabbering away. Richelle was still there, too, pointing and talking as fast as her tongue would allow.

"I was really being careful, Mrs. Ervin, honest I was," Richelle said. "She just twisted her head around and came right out of her collar and then she just took off, and I don't know where she went—"

Austin puffed with excitement. "She did," he kept repeating. "She did, she did, she did."

Jeremy's breath caught in his throat. Was Duchess gone again?

"And then when she came back"—Richelle shook her

head, and her dark eyes went wide—"she had this *thing* with her."

"A bone, Mommy," Austin said. "A big, huge, 'normous bone."

Jeremy was smiling again. It sounded as if Duchess was safely home after all.

"I've never seen such a gross thing in my whole life," Richelle said.

Quinn snorted. "You say that all the time."

"And she won't let go of it, Mrs. Ervin," Richelle said, ignoring her brother.

"Well, there's probably no harm done, and I know you did your best, so don't worry." Jeremy's mother opened her purse, pulled out a bill, and pressed it into Richelle's hand. "Thanks for watching Austin," she said wearily. "You can go on now, while Quinn's here to walk you home."

Brother and sister scowled at each other. "Okay," Richelle said. "But Duchess is in the backyard, and maybe you ought to take a look or something."

Jeremy's mother nodded and took Austin by the hand, and Jeremy went, too, to stare over the chain-link fence at Duchess and her treasure, which now lay beside her. No one spoke, not even Austin.

Then Mrs. Ervin cleared her throat. "Well, I'll have to say I agree with Richelle. I've never seen anything quite like it. I don't have any idea what kind of animal it might be from—and cut all ragged like that. What butcher would sell such a thing?"

"Duchess looks really happy," Jeremy said. Even so, his mother gave him careful directions for taking the bone away and shutting the dog in the laundry room for the night in case she should be sick.

Jeremy did as he was told, getting old newspapers to wrap around the bone so he wouldn't touch it and be covered with germs, as his mother predicted. His dog watched him but made no protest, although she paced along the fence as he carried her prize to the tall garbage can and dropped it in.

Duchess spent a comfortable night on the rug in front of the dryer. It was Jeremy who had trouble sleeping. All the events of the day kept crowding back into his head. And he worried, as he twisted this way and that on his bed, that there might have been something toxic about the bone Duchess had found. His hand, the one that had carried it, had a faint little tingle now. Or at least he thought so. He didn't know what it could be. Maybe he was allergic to bones or something. Tomorrow he would have to talk it over with Quinn.

CHAPTER 3

Ulf

In the days after the feast, Ulf burned with questions that he dared not ask in the queen's household and that brought no answer in the wizard's hut.

"Do you know the one they call Gudrun the Fair?" he asked Old Berta. "Do you know, is she a princess? What place does she come from?"

Berta did not even look up from the tiny dry leaves she was grinding into powder on the hollowed stone. "Ah," she said softly, "*that* one. If the chance comes to you, be kind." And that was all.

He thought of asking Gudrun herself to explain what she had said at the feast's head table, but he was hardly bold enough to speak first. Nor was there any opportunity, for now that the war troop had returned, Gudrun never toiled along the path with her water jar. Instead, she stayed among the noblewomen. On fair days, they warmed themselves in the autumn sun at the edge of the queen's orchard, where they sat on cushions and fleeces, chattering over their needlework. He began to watch her there, hoping for some sign that would tell him whether she spoke truly about danger to come.

Ulf's usual path from the scullery to the stream provided no view of the orchard, so he chose another way. This track was narrower, steeper, longer. Its advantage was that it came out of the forest's edge very near to the queen's precious fruit trees, looping out around their gnarled forms on its way to the keep. There was a risk, Ulf knew, in using that path, for it was the one frequented by the wood gatherers, who were older and bigger, and who had already given him plenty of reason for caution.

He meant to be wary, to step off the path and hide among the branches if he saw them coming. There was no trouble the first day, but on the second he fell to thinking about the way Gudrun was sitting so silent among her companions, and as he thought, he let down his guard. He was quite near to the place where the path left the trees.

"Wizard's boy!" They were on him in a moment, three of them, swarming up from behind to push and smack him. "Get yourself off our track!"

Ulf made himself small, pulling away from the blows. He tried in vain to keep the water jar in his grasp, but someone stronger twisted it out of his arms and held it above him.

"Puli!" he cried, recognizing the boy. "Stop!" But Puli tipped the jar anyway, and all the water came spilling over Ulf's head. The boy laughed and gave the empty jar a little toss. Sopping as he was and suddenly cold, Ulf did not step away in time. He felt the heavy vessel scrape his face, and then the thud of it against his chest that made him fall.

For a moment, Ulf could not breathe. Then, dimly, he began to hear the jeers and laughter of the others. When he struggled to sit up, pain wrapped around his middle like a sash.

Puli leaned over him. "Why are you here anyway?" he demanded. "No one as puny as you uses this steep track, and no one carries water jars the long way around."

Ulf could not think of a lie. "I keep watch," he mumbled.

"What are you watching, little outlander?" Puli's leer turned into a snarl. "Are you some sort of spy?"

No answer came into Ulf's mind. He cringed as the other boys began to laugh and taunt him.

"Spy!"

"Spy!"

"Secret warrior!"

"A spy for the yellow-haired girl!"

In the sudden silence, Ulf held his breath.

Puli leaned closer still. "Is that it, little outlander? Are you sworn to her service instead of the king's?"

Ulf tried to shake his head, but it barely moved.

"I brought wood to the feast, wizard's boy," Puli said slowly, "and I saw you whispering with her. Like a traitor! You and your foreign hair like hers!" Without warning, he reached into Ulf's tousle of golden strands and held on with a vicious, twisting grip. Ulf thought he would faint. He hoped he would faint, to take the pain away.

"Prince Ar won't like to have anyone plotting with that yellow-haired girl," Puli said, growling the words right into his face. "You best be careful or the prince will sic his dog on you, boy!"

Deep down inside Ulf, beyond the hurting, something came to life. He managed to come up into a crouch with his feet under him.

"I would not be afraid of the prince's dog," Ulf said defiantly. "I have . . . my own dog."

"Liar!" Puli released Ulf's hair with a final yank that pulled him upright.

"Proof!" cried another of the boys. "Where did you get a dog?"

Ulf swayed on unsteady legs. He had no idea what else to say.

"Where?" The boy who demanded proof grabbed Ulf's

arm and bent it behind his back. "Dogs stay close to their masters," he said. "So call yours and we'll have a look."

"No!" said Ulf.

"Call for it!" Puli insisted. When Ulf did not comply, the boy who held his arm began to lean his weight against it.

It was more than Ulf could bear. He took a breath and tried to pucker his lips, but the whistling sound he made was so faint it scarcely reached his own ears. What he heard clearly was a snapping of twigs in the underbrush along the path, and then a low snarl. At that moment Puli gave a shout, and his companion released Ulf so abruptly that he went spinning back to the ground.

"Wolf!" screamed Puli, leaping over Ulf's form sprawled on the path. "Wolf! Wolf!" The other boys took up the shout as they dashed for the orchard and the keep beyond, and soon their voices were joined by the shrieks of fleeing women as wood gatherers and ladies in waiting ran for their lives together.

Ulf lay without moving on the path, his eyes closed. He fought to make his mind work, to think how he could escape. Should he run? Could he make his body do it? For one terrifying moment, nothing happened. Then suddenly he heard the animal panting and felt the warmth of its breath on his injured cheek. Ulf gasped and in spite of himself opened his eyes to see the beast. The scream on his lips turned to no sound at all. The eyes that looked back into his were gray as a winter sky. It was the dog—his dog, from the ravine. All at once she was licking his cheek and his nose and his neck, and he was laughing and babbling and rolling on the path like a person gone mad.

"Lie still!" a high voice called. "Lie still, and I'll drive it away!"

"No!" Ulf found his feet and stood with his hand on the dog's head, steadying himself. Gudrun the Fair was running toward them with an applewood branch held like a club in both her hands.

"There is no harm!" he cried.

She stopped, breathing hard, and then slowly she smiled. "A dog!" she marveled. "How tame for such a huge creature—and how beautiful."

Ulf stroked the soft hair beneath his hand. If she had thought it was a wolf, she had great courage. He tried to smile, although his face felt stiff and misshapen.

Gudrun dropped her eyes and let the length of applewood tumble to the ground. "What name do you call her?"

The question took him by surprise, and he hesitated. "M-m-magic," he stammered finally. The dog's tail waved. "Her name is Magic."

The young woman's eyes went wide, and she took a small step backward. "Ah," she said. "A dog with a dangerous name. It's the wizard's, then."

Ulf opened his mouth to contradict her, but he did not

know how to explain. The mention of the wizard reminded him of the gravity of his situation. Had he not just disobeyed everything that Harket had told him? He shrugged and gave Gudrun no answer. And then, although it broke his heart, and although he could not guess the outcome, he made the signal that meant "go home" to the hounds in the queen's kennel. The dog turned obediently and trotted away into the forest. "I—I am not allowed to tell about this dog," he said.

Gudrun nodded. "I would not reveal your secret."

Ulf was grateful, but some of the spirit went out of him as he watched the dog go. He began to notice how his head throbbed and how every movement wakened a new pain. All his cuts and bumps and scratches called out to him. He knew he had to hobble back to the kitchen and face the cook with no water and no jar, for now he was not even able to pick up the vessel and carry it.

The girl had been staring at his wounds, and she began to shake her head. "They are a pack of louts," she said softly, handing him the applewood club to lean on. She turned and hurried back along the path to the orchard.

It was not a day totally lacking in good fortune, Ulf realized later, for the punishment he expected from the cook never came. His story reached the scullery before his poor, bruised body did. The cook was not willing to lay his hand on a boy who was said to have been eaten by a golden wolf and then, soon after, reappeared in the flesh. A boy like that, a wizard's boy, should have a sweetmeat and take himself to his bed and let his bruises heal and come back to his tasks another day.

The cook's generosity only hastened the moment Ulf dreaded most. Step by aching step, he made his way to the wizard's hut, where Old Berta clucked over his wounds and soothed them with ointments and silently bound up the ones that bled.

"I should speak to the wizard," he whispered when she was finished.

She shook her head. "Harket is gone on a journey," she said.

He took a breath; his chest felt lighter.

"One of the king's men came," Berta went on, "and sat on the bench where you sit now and begged my husband to risk his life."

Ulf shuddered. "How?" he said. "Where has he gone?"

"To track a golden wolf."

"No!" Ulf leaped to his feet and, in his weakness, would have fallen if Berta had not caught him in her wrinkled hands. "There is no golden wolf!" he cried. His voice was shaking, his body was shaking. It seemed to him that the hut itself shook. "There is no wolf," he repeated, and he could not tell if his words were loud or soft. "The dog came," he said. "The dog I told you of, before. It chased away the ones who beat me and they called it a wolf and made everyone afraid." Tears came down his cheeks now, glistening here and there in Berta's healing ointment.

The old woman lowered the boy to the bench and brought her crooked nose within a hair's breadth of his battered cheek. "Did you touch that animal again?"

"She touched me first," he said. "There was nothing I could do to help it. I was fallen on the ground, and she came running to me and licked me, and—" He closed his mouth, and his eyes, remembering.

Old Berta loosed her grip on him and turned away, fetching out a jar from behind the corner curtain. "Tell me the names of the lads who hurt you," she said, and her voice was so grim he could not refuse. He hoped she would not punish them, would not put a spell on them, for they would suspect he had a hand in it and beat him again for revenge. And he hoped Harket would not find the dog.

"Berta," he said miserably, "if Harket finds that dog—"

"Tut," she said, cutting him off. "Harket will know what to do."

"But—" When Ulf opened his mouth to plead the dog's case, Old Berta spooned something into it.

"Swallow!" she demanded, and he obeyed without thinking.

Within a heartbeat, he felt that he was on fire, that he had turned to smoke and steam. He tried to get to his feet. He had to find water. But Berta held him firmly by the front of his tunic and breathed words into his face. Gradually the burning faded from him, and she led him to his sleeping mat.

"What did you do?" He formed each word carefully. "What medicine was that you gave me?"

"Not medicine," she said. "A gift. I gave you the charm of language—for your ears and for your lips."

He shook his head in befuddlement, a small motion that left him dizzy with pain.

"Now to sleep," the old woman said, touching his shoulder with a gentle hand.

He eased himself down onto the familiar pad of wool. "Why a charm?" he asked. His voice was groggy now, and slow. "Why a charm for me?"

Old Berta scowled at nothing, her face far above him. "With creatures like that," she said, "you never can tell. You never can tell what will travel with them."

The boy fell into sleep then and dreamed the first of many feverish dreams, where ghostly figures leaped like trolls and shouted on the high path above the ravine while impossible drums clattered on without ceasing.

❖ Jeremy

Duchess was grounded. No more walks, by order of Jeremy's father. "I'll bring home a harness for her," he promised when he went to work on Monday, "one she can't pull out of. *Then* you can take her out in the neighborhood again. But not until."

Jeremy had heard his mother describing the bone to his father. *"Huge!"* she had said. "I've never seen anything *like* it!" So Duchess's punishment came as no surprise. But that first day Mr. Ervin had to work late, and on the second there was a traffic tie-up that kept him away from the pet store, and by then it was the middle of the week and Duchess still had to pace along the backyard fence for her exercise.

When Jeremy got home from school, he spent a long time tossing sticks for her to catch, even though there was not much room to chase after them in the Ervins' backyard. "Good dog," he said again and again. "Good pup." He put her through most of the obedience routine they had learned together—sit, stay, lie down, come, shake hands— and rewarded her with cheese treats, her favorite. "Do you want me to play some more with you, beautiful Duchess?" He leaned over until he was nose to nose with the dog, and she nuzzled him, snuffling up to his ear and then down to the jacket pocket where he carried the treats.

"Jeremy!" Austin's voice rose over the banging of the door to the screen porch. "Here I am! I'm home! My turn to play with Duchess now!"

"Huh-*uh*!" Jeremy said. Actually, he didn't really care. He thought Quinn might be home by this time; the middle school was in session half an hour later every day than his own school, but Quinn didn't have far to walk.

"Duchess is in doggie jail," Austin announced as the dog loped toward him. "See? Look, Jeremy! I'm the guard. Look at me!"

"Okay, Austin." Jeremy had to smile at the way Austin was standing, his arms stiff at his sides and his chest puffed out. Duchess weighed almost twice as much as his little brother. "Take good care of your prisoner," Jeremy said. "Make sure she gets her exercise."

"March, dog!" shouted Austin. "March!" The dog sat down and wagged her long plume of a tail, sweeping dry leaves from side to side.

Jeremy escaped into the house just as the phone rang. It was Quinn, wanting him to come over. His mother was shuffling through a pile of books on one end of the kitchen counter. She looked at her watch, frowning, and held up one finger. "One hour," she said. "Have you seen my book? I'm looking for *Gudrun's Tale*. Green cover."

Jeremy rolled his eyes and shook his head, then ducked into the coat closet to finish his conversation.

"It's okay, Quinn," he said, "but I don't have much time. I'm going to bring, like, maybe just a dozen of my really good fighters and we can play the quick way." He tried to find his old sweatshirt by touch, but instead, his hand fell on a Union Army cap that his Uncle Mike had brought him from a Civil War battlefield. "What I think we should do today," he said, the idea traveling straight from his fingers to his brain, "is, like, be in uniform ourselves. I'm going to bring this great hat." Jeremy took it down and stuffed it under his school jacket. Not that he would care if anyone saw him wearing it, he thought. "You must have something there you can use."

"It'll just hold us up, Jeremy." Quinn's voice came through in a mumble.

Jeremy pushed the channel button on the phone several times to clear the sound and to give the other boy a moment to think. "Come on, Quinn," he said. "Let's."

"Well, okay. Maybe. Meet me down at the far end of my street."

Outside again. That would be perfect, Jeremy thought. He rushed to his room to load his pockets with warriors and then on to meet his friend. But Quinn wasn't there, and Jeremy had to wait for what seemed like a long time.

When Quinn finally arrived, he was jogging, and he barely slowed down to speak.

"Come on, Jeremy," he panted. "We'll go on down to the fort. It'll be great!"

Jeremy hesitated. What if his mother found out? Or his father?

But Quinn wasn't waiting for him. "Are you coming or not?" he called, and so Jeremy followed. They had gone only a little way through the trees when Quinn stopped. Jeremy pulled out his hat and put it on.

Quinn laughed. "Pretty lame," he said. "But how about

this?" He stripped off the floppy black football jersey that covered him from neck to knees.

Jeremy gasped. "Awesome!" he said. Quinn had come up with the perfect thing. He was wearing a huge T-shirt painted to look like a tunic of chain mail.

"My dad wore it to a party one year," Quinn explained, turning to show off the back, where a fake wound was splattered with red. "Cool, huh?"

Jeremy shook his head in wondering admiration. "You're the best," he said.

Just then, from the narrow street below, a voice shouted, "Hey, who's up there?" Jeremy saw two bicycles coming slowly along, bicycles coasting to a halt. Both riders were boys, but Jeremy didn't know them. One had a football, and as they stopped, they began to toss it back and forth between them.

"DaSilva! DaSilva, is that you?"

A look that Jeremy couldn't name came up on Quinn's face.

"Who are they?" Jeremy whispered, following his friend into a sudden crouch.

"Eighth graders," muttered Quinn, struggling to get the T-shirt up over his head. "They'll think this stuff is stupid," he said, kicking the wonderful fake chain mail under a bush.

"Quinn!" Jeremy's heart began to beat fast as a jackhammer. "What's *that*?" He pointed. Around Quinn's waist was an unfamiliar belt, from which hung a short leather scabbard. A wooden handle inlaid with metal showed above it.

"DaSilva?" The voice rose up again from below. "Where'd you go?"

"It's just part of the costume, sort of," Quinn whispered to Jeremy as he fumbled with the belt buckle.

"That's gotta be real, Quinn," Jeremy said. "That's not plastic!"

"Shhh! Not so loud." Belt and scabbard fell into the leaves around their feet. "It's something that used to belong to my Dad's grandfather," Quinn whispered. "But it's mine now, sort of."

"No way!" Jeremy felt a mix of admiration, envy, and doubt. Mostly doubt. "That can't be yours!"

"Well, Dad says it is! It's *going* to be mine. Except he still takes care of it. He keeps it with that other stuff in his souvenir chest."

Jeremy's mouth fell open. He couldn't believe that Quinn had dared to unlock the big black box in Mr. DaSilva's den. He had been dying to see what was inside ever since Quinn had first told him it was filled with old, old things. But the box was always locked, and Mr. DaSilva had cautioned them both away from it, time after time.

"DaSilva!" The voice from below was impatient. "Don't you want to go through a couple of drills with us?"

"Listen, Jeremy," Quinn said, looking perplexed, "I ought to go with those guys for a little while. Alone, okay? They play in a weekend league and everything."

"But we were—" Jeremy didn't know what to say. He looked down at the belt; it had coiled itself like a snake among the leaves. "And you can't leave this—"

Quinn sighed. "Can't you be the weapons master and it's your job to take care of this stuff? Please?" He pulled his football jersey back on and stood up. "Guys!" he shouted. "Up here! I'm on my way down!"

"That isn't fair, Quinn!" Jeremy's temper, which was hard to rouse, began to flicker deep inside him. "What am I supposed to do?"

"You'll figure it out," Quinn said. "You always do." And he began to make his way down into the ravine.

Jeremy sat silent for a moment. Then he reached for the handle that stuck out of the fallen scabbard and pulled. He caught his breath at the sight of the gleaming blade, two-sided, a dagger. It was no longer than the big slicing knives in the wood block on his mother's counter, yet no kitchen knife had ever filled him with such feeling. He thought it was beautiful, so straight and true. It reminded him of all the tiny weapons his ancient warriors carried. But there was something fearsome about this one; it made his mouth dry to look at it. He wished he didn't have it in his hand, in his keeping.

Jeremy stared at the dagger for a long time before his

sensible side came awake. What he ought to do, he thought, was return it to Mr. DaSilva's souvenir chest. He knew where to find the emergency key to Quinn's house, but the key for the box was another matter. Mr. DaSilva wouldn't be home, although Richelle probably would. No use trying to get away with anything when there was such a champion squealer around.

Jeremy sighed. Returning the knife would have to be Quinn's job. He could just leave it here in the leaves for Quinn to get later, but somehow he felt responsible for taking better care of it than that. Something this old and this beautiful might be worth a lot of money. For sure, it was too special to be lost on this hillside.

He considered whether he should take the weapon home with him. If his father found out, it would mean giant trouble; and he couldn't begin to imagine the fuss his mother would make: "Where did you get that? Why do you have it? What's it doing here?" She hadn't even let him have the rubber sword that came with his pirate costume the Halloween that he was seven. And what if Austin happened to find this dagger? He could hurt himself. Jeremy sighted along the edge of the blade. Austin could hurt himself badly.

Finally Jeremy pulled the chain-mail T-shirt from the bush where Quinn had put it and spread it carefully to one side. It made him sad, such a great costume going to waste. Next he blew his breath across the dagger and polished it carefully on his jacket sleeve before replacing it in the scabbard. He coiled the belt into the smallest possible space and wrapped everything in the shirt.

Jeremy stood up. Quinn and the other boys were nowhere in sight. He picked up his lumpy package and began to make his way across the steep hillside, searching for the alders that hid the little hollow Quinn called a fort. It was harder to find than he had expected, and there was almost no light at all coming through the bushes when he moved the flat stones at the back and scratched a shallow hole where they had been.

"There!" he said to himself when he had pressed his bundle into the dirt and replaced the stones. It occurred to him that he was having an adventure that would fit right into one of their battles, but it wasn't any fun without Quinn. It wasn't fair for his best friend and partner in arms to desert him like this; it wasn't right somehow.

All the way home it bothered him, and when he got to the house, he expected to be in trouble for being late. For a moment he thought he saw his mother waiting for him at the top of the steps. She would have plenty to say to him, too, although there was no way for her to know just how many ways he had disobeyed her. But when he came closer he was shocked to see that it was Duchess sitting on the front porch, free as air. She came to greet him silently, licking the hand he held out to her.

"What are you doing out here?" Jeremy whispered.

Duchess was a better friend than Quinn any day, he thought. And a good dog, too, to be outside the fence but not running away. When they slipped around to the side of the house, Jeremy almost tripped over Austin's tricycle, which lay on its side just at the gate. The gate was ajar, and Jeremy felt sure Austin had opened it but hadn't closed it right since he still had trouble reaching the latch. Then Duchess must have come along and pushed her way outside.

"Maybe they haven't missed you yet," he said to the dog. "Or me, either." Jeremy carried the tricycle to its regular parking place in the backyard, double-checked the gate latch to make sure it had shut, and then opened the screen-porch door for Duchess. He could see Austin in the family room, eyes riveted to the television, twitching to the rhythm of cartoon music. Beyond the counter at the edge of the kitchen, his mother turned from the sink to the stove and back again. She wore a pencil behind one ear and a faraway look that meant she was thinking about her project instead of whatever was in the skillet. His father wasn't home yet. All systems normal. No panic. Jeremy went into the house with Duchess, relieved. Maybe it was only in the ravine that things somehow seemed amiss.

CHAPTER 4

❖ *Ulf*

Ulf bore the marks of his clash with Puli and the others for many days, long after he was strong enough to take up his duties again in the queen's household. He was ill at ease when he returned to his tasks, both because he did not wish to display his scars and because his mind kept settling on the wizard, who had not yet returned. What if Harket had found the dog? And what if he had harmed her? Ulf kept to himself more than ever, hiding his thoughts as well as his wounds. He used the old path to the stream, always careful to take cover along the way if he should hear or see any sign of another traveler.

He was so successful in his solitary ways, and the others were so willing to leave him alone in the aftermath of his encounter with the golden wolf, that he failed to keep up with important news of the day. So it was that when the war troop rode out for one last raid before the snows of winter, no gossip had prepared him for their departure. If they had not made such a clatter in leaving, and if Ludwig's banner had not flown on so tall a staff, he might have missed entirely the moment of their going.

As it was, he was making a trip for water when he saw the troop on its way. A shaft of sun broke through the mist as foot soldiers and horsemen skirted the rocks along the path. They followed the stream in the ravine down toward the river, the river that led at last to the sea. He watched them from the shelter of a thicket upstream, and then, as he started off to fill his jar, he realized that he was not yet quite alone.

One of the riders sat his mount on the high path across the stream, his outline blurred in the morning's haze. Ulf scuttled backward into the thicket as the horseman gave a shout and began to wind his way down, letting the animal find its own footing. They had almost reached the water before Ulf recognized the rider. It was Prince Ar.

Ulf's breath caught in his throat. Prince Ar was coming for him, he was sure. Puli must have gone to the prince and told him that story about spying, Ulf thought, and he shivered. Spies were put to the sword, or worse, and he could see that Ar carried his weapon. And I have nothing, Ulf thought. He will kill me!

But the prince rode through the stream and past Ulf's hiding place without stopping—without even seeing, Ulf decided. He let out the huge breath he had been holding and wiggled deeper into the brush, turning to follow Ar with his eyes. The horse had gone only a few steps farther when the prince reined it to a halt and dismounted.

"I have been searching for you," Prince Ar said to some-one Ulf could not see. His voice was patient. "I come to bid you farewell."

At that moment Ulf caught sight of Princess Orrun, who came around a bend in the path followed by two of the housemaids and, finally, Gudrun the Fair. Each carried a bundle of vines bright with berries, the same as Old Berta took pains to gather in the fall of the year.

"Oh, brother Ar!" cried the young princess. "I wish you need not go!" And she chattered on about this and that until Ulf began to wonder if his poor, cramped muscles would turn to stone and leave him forever bent. But in a moment the prince hushed her, and made his good-bye, and sent her on along the path with the housemaids.

"You stay," said Prince Ar to Gudrun. Some of the patience had gone out of his voice.

Ulf wished that he could see her face, but the prince and his horse now filled all the space between the branches where he dared to peer out.

"When I am home again," said Prince Ar to the girl, "I

shall take you as my bride, just as the king and my mother have planned."

Silence. A bird trilled some way off, and the horse whickered softly; but Ulf heard no sound at all from Gudrun.

"Say just one word and you shall wear our crown!" Ar's voice rose, although he did not shout.

"I say one word, and it is no!" she said clearly. "I have said from the beginning that I cannot be wedded to you!"

"I have been more than patient."

There was a sigh from Gudrun. "You have," she said softly. "But your mother has not. She treats me ill."

"I have cautioned the queen to think of you as her own daughter, whether you give her reason to or not. I have been nothing but kind to you, Gudrun. Have you forgotten that once I saved your life?"

Ulf heard the girl whisper something in return, but her voice fell so low that he could not be sure the words were ones of gratitude.

Prince Ar took a step toward her. "Pledge yourself," he urged. "Pledge yourself to me. Wear our crown and we will be happy together!"

"I cannot!" Her voice broke. "I will not!"

She moved, and Ulf could see that she warded off the prince's advance with the vines she carried, so that he could not reach through them to touch her. "I am promised to another, and you well know it," she said.

"Betrothed to Erik of Zirn! By my dead father's oath and by my own heart!"

"Pah!" Prince Ar spat on the ground. "So I have heard! But where is he now, this prince who once claimed you? Like as not, he lies dead on some far shore. And I, Armut, I am here, and you are in my holdings now. These lands will all be mine! And it is my queen you will be, and not his!"

Ar's voice had grown so loud that Ulf trembled, making him afraid that the thicket would rattle and give him away. He wished that he had courage enough to burst up out of it and run to the girl's defense. He could hear her weeping softly, and he wanted to comfort her, but he could not.

"Leave me now!" the prince ordered. "Go! Do not keep Orrun waiting. And remember that when I am home again, I will be patient no more." He let her pass, although Ulf could see how he held his arms tight to his sides, with clenched fists.

Ulf dared not turn to watch Gudrun out of sight, but he listened as the sound of her footsteps faded. At last he heard the gentle echo of girls' voices, then silence. And now, thought Ulf, Prince Ar would swing up on his horse and ride off to take his place beside the king at the head of the war troop. Then Ulf could stand and stretch the cramps from his body and breathe fresh air to clear his mind of all he had heard to disturb it.

The prince did not oblige. He stayed on the path beside

the stream for some time, pacing back and forth and muttering at the ground. Ulf had held himself in a crouch so long he had lost the feeling in his feet, and he knew he could not move. Thus paralyzed, he felt great fear as the prince unsheathed his sword and began to swing it with all his power. *Slash!* A clump of tall brown grass went flying. Had the prince seen him after all? His stomach churned. *Slash!* The end of a fir branch bobbled and fell. Did Ar think him a spy? It was all the boy could do to keep from retching. *Slash!* A tiny brown stick from the top of the thicket tumbled down and lodged in Ulf's hair. A sound of terror escaped his lips; he could not hold it back.

Prince Ar stood with the sword held aloft in both his hands as if to strike the thicket a killing blow. But the prince's eyes were closed, and he was beyond hearing. "Erik! Erik!" he was shouting. "Erik of Zirn!" But just when Ulf thought there was no way for him to escape the prince's blade, Ar shuddered and turned away. In a moment the weapon was safely in its sheath and Prince Ar was on his mount, splashing downstream after the others.

Ulf could not find the strength to climb out of his hiding place; his limbs were too numb and weak. It was the sound of a dog's barking, far away, that finally brought him to his feet. But watch as he might, no dog appeared, and he returned to his tasks with more worries than he could count.

❖ *Jeremy*

No one else gets up *this* early on Saturday, Jeremy thought with satisfaction. This was the morning he and Quinn were going to retrieve Quinn's knife or dagger or whatever it was before his father found out it was missing. Quinn was going to put it back where he found it, and that would be the end of it. They had straightened everything out on the phone and made all their plans. Richelle always slept late on Saturdays, and so did Mr. DaSilva, so that part would be fine. It was only at his own house where things might go wrong.

When Jeremy crept to the kitchen to get a bowl of cereal, he heard the whine of his mother's printer in the study and the low singsong of her voice, reading back to herself whatever it was she was writing. *"The queen said to her son, 'Leave the girl with me, and I will train her'*—er—*'teach her.' . . . And he said, 'Be gentle,' but the queen had a taste for punishment and made her carry water like a common servant. And so . . . "*

Jeremy couldn't tell if his mother had started to work so early because her project was going well or because it wasn't. Whichever way, it was best not to disturb her. All he needed was to have a little breakfast and to leave the house without anyone noticing, and at first he thought he could do it.

But just as Jeremy opened the refrigerator for milk, Duchess streaked past him and began to bark at the door that led to the screen porch.

"No! Shhh!" Jeremy tried to shout and whisper at the same time, but it came out louder than he planned. Duchess barked even harder, almost blocking out the muted *wham! wham!* that had roused her.

"Quinn!" Jeremy opened the door and hurried to the end of the screen porch, where the other boy waited to be let in and now Duchess waited to be let out. "What are you doing here? You were supposed to wait for me! You'll wake everybody up!"

Quinn shrugged. "I thought we wanted to get this over with before anyone came to the ravine," he said. Duchess made a quick circle around the yard and came bounding back to the porch, where she licked Quinn just as happily as she did Jeremy.

"I haven't even had my cereal yet," Jeremy whispered, leading the way back into the kitchen.

"Me, either," Quinn said, rubbing his stomach. "What kind do you have?"

Jeremy turned to open the cupboard door and saw his parents staring at them.

"What are you doing here at this hour, Quinn?" Mr. Ervin's voice was sleepy and slow. "Did you spend the night?"

Quinn shook his head. "Uh . . . not this time."

"So, then, Jeremy," said his mother, "what's going on?"

"Nothing, Mom. Quinn and I just thought we'd get an early start . . . you know, with the warriors and everything." Jeremy fastened his eyes on the neat row of cereal boxes, as if it took all of a person's attention to tell cornflakes from puffed rice. Duchess began to circle the family room with a chew toy that whistled eerily every time she moved her jaws.

"Austin is still sleeping," Jeremy's mother said with a note of warning in her voice.

Mr. Ervin yawned. "And some of the rest of us wish we were."

"Certain others of us are having fits with this project," Jeremy's mother said, "which was due last week. So we were hoping for peace and quiet, certainly until the sun was up! At *least*!"

Jeremy looked at the floor. Maybe Quinn wouldn't notice how funny his mother sounded when she was in a fuss about her work.

"We'll go out just as soon as we've had breakfast," Quinn promised, smiling as he moved toward the refrigerator.

Jeremy saw his parents exchange a look.

"Tell you what," his father said. "How about a backyard breakfast this morning? Take some of those granola bars and a couple of juice boxes or something, and come on back in when it's time for reasonable people to be up and about on a Saturday."

"Okay," Jeremy said. "Sweet." This was turning out better than he could have hoped.

"Don't forget your jacket," his mother said. "It will be damp out there with all the fog."

Duchess chewed mightily on her squeaker toy.

"And take this dog out with you," his father directed. "She's a pain this morning, plain and simple."

"Okay," Jeremy said again, more slowly. Duchess might complicate things. He looked at Quinn. "What if she barks and carries on outside?"

"No problem," Quinn said. "We can take her over to my house."

Jeremy beamed. Of course! They needed an excuse to go to Quinn's house after they had been to the ravine, anyway. "Is that okay, Dad? We can take her around for a walk on the way, so she'll be settled when we get there."

"Fine, fine," said Mr. Ervin, turning toward the stairs. "Make sure you use the new harness."

"Thank you, boys," Jeremy's mother said. "It will make my day if Austin can sleep until Richelle comes." She disappeared into the study while Quinn rolled his eyes.

"If Richelle comes over here, it will sure make *my* day," he said. He loaded his pockets with carry-out breakfast while Jeremy pulled at the movable straps on the dog's harness. It took awhile to figure out which part snapped where. Duchess was wary until Quinn slipped her a piece of granola bar. After that, Jeremy lifted her right front leg through the final loop, adjusted it, and they were ready to go.

Outside, the air was cool and thick with mist. Duchess used her nose to check for squirrels, tugging forward against the harness. "Ow, dog," Jeremy complained. "You're hurting my arm."

Quinn started toward the far end of Jeremy's street, the dead end, where they could just make out the outline of old Mrs. Ramey's house. It faced them, with its back gardens rambling on to the edge of the ravine. "Let's go this way," he said. "It's quickest."

Jeremy frowned. "Mrs. Ramey complains to my mom all the time about people taking shortcuts through her yard."

"She'll be asleep now. And besides, we won't hurt anything." Quinn's walk turned into a trot. Duchess loped after him, pulling Jeremy along.

"Why do we have to hurry so, Quinn? Don't we have time?"

"I want to get this done," Quinn said over his shoulder, and Jeremy understood. Quinn's father was going to be really bent out of shape if he found out, and besides, they were using up perfectly good battle time this way.

Suddenly Jeremy had a troubling thought. "You aren't in a hurry because of those eighth-grade guys, are you? You don't have to meet them somewhere or something?"

Quinn slowed his pace. "No!" He made a sound of disgust. "I told you on the phone, they're losers!"

"Oh," said Jeremy, hoping for more explanation. But by then they were busy watching their feet as they wound their way carefully along one side of the overgrown Ramey garden. Everything seemed ghostly in the murky air.

"The fort's over this way," Quinn said. "Come on." Jeremy tried to hurry, but Duchess stopped to sniff at so many things along the way that he soon fell behind. The harness kept her from getting away all right; but when she stopped and planted her feet, there was nothing to do but wait.

"It's right down there! See the tops of those bushes?" Quinn pointed. "Let me take the dog," he said. "I'm stronger. I can handle her better than you."

No, you can't, Jeremy thought. "Come on, Duchess," he said, but Duchess took her time, working her long muzzle farther and farther into a clump of damp leaves.

"Listen, Jeremy, I could keep her up here while you go down and get the knife," Quinn suggested as Jeremy caught up to him.

"But it's your knife," Jeremy said. "You ought to be the one who gets it." He smiled. "You know, like recapturing it from the enemy or something." He looked cautiously over the edge of the bank. Hardly anything looked familiar in this light.

"Yeah, but you're the one that buried it," Quinn said. "I don't know exactly where to look. I could be, like, King

What's-His-Name—I don't remember, but it began with an L. And you could be the scout, and—"

Jeremy grinned. "And I come across this little fort place, just the way I did the other day, and in it I find this terrific dagger, and I bring it to my king, and he gives me a big reward."

"Yeah!" said Quinn, reaching for the dog's leash.

Silently, Jeremy considered the advantages of keeping Duchess out of the ravine. Number one, there wouldn't be as many burrs to brush out of her coat, and that was a big thing. "Okay, Your Highness. Here's the dog," he said. "But make sure you hang on to her so she doesn't follow me and get all covered with stuff."

"Right!" Quinn wrapped the heavy leash around his hand to keep Duchess close to his side. He looked up and down the ravine. "There's something creepy about this fog," he said.

But Jeremy was already busy making his way down to the alder bushes that marked the fort. The closer he got to them, the easier they were to see. Fog was like that, he reminded himself, and it encouraged him. There was the entrance. He pushed the bushes aside. Soon he would have the knife, and Quinn would return it to his father's souvenir chest, and then it could be just a regular Saturday again.

Just at that moment Duchess began barking furiously. Jeremy recognized it as her squirrel-alert bark, sharp and frenzied. He looked up the hillside in time to see her come hurtling down, still attached to Quinn, who was bumping and sliding along behind.

"Duchess!" Jeremy lunged and managed to stop her. She barked once more as the little furry creature streaked away over a rock and into the fog.

"Look what you did to me, dog!" Quinn untangled himself from the leash and rubbed the welts on his wrist. Duchess panted.

Jeremy shook his head. "I'll hold her this time," he said, "and I'll tell you exactly where the knife is, and you can get it."

They turned back toward the fort.

"Huh!" said Quinn. "I thought it was right here."

"It was." Jeremy forgot to breathe. The mist was clearing, was streaked with sunlight. The bushes that marked the fort were completely gone. The trees he saw were autumn trees, but they were not the ones that had surrounded him just moments before. He could hear the stream below, although he knew that the sluggish thread of water at the foot of the ravine made no sound. Out of the corner of his eye, he could see the deep color of an evergreen forest stretching far up a steep mountain slope.

"Quinn!" He had trouble with his voice. "Look around! This isn't our— This isn't the right—" He was trying to be sensible, but here was something he couldn't be sensible about. He knew for a fact that there weren't any mountains at all within a hundred miles of his house. Ms. Hernandez had made sure his whole class knew that for their last geography test.

"This is weird," Quinn said under his breath. "What happened? Where are we?"

"I don't know." Jeremy could barely get the words out. "It's a ravine, sort of, but it's all different. We're in the wrong place, somehow."

Duchess tested the air with her nose and began to wag her tail. That made Jeremy feel a little better, but not much. Suddenly, above the gurgle of the stream, he heard an unexpected sound—*clop-clop, clop-clop, clop-clop.*

"Shhh!" he said to Quinn, while he reached under the dog's harness for the collar she always wore. In an emergency he could twist it just enough to keep her quiet.

"Wow!" Quinn's breath was almost a word. Below them, coming their way along the edge of the stream, was a lone horseman. He was dressed like an ancient warrior. His tunic and the saddle pad of his mount bore the marks of royalty. A sword in its sheath was near to the rider's hand. He looked up once and then pressed on, moving into the stream. The horse's hooves made a great splash that sparkled and fell as the rider went out of sight.

Jeremy looked at Quinn, whose face was paper white.

"Did you see a guy on a horse just now?" Quinn whispered.

Jeremy swallowed. "Let's get out of here."

"How?"

"I don't know!" Jeremy shivered. "Let's just try to go back up the way we came. Come on, Duchess, let's go home!"

After that, it was easy. They both held the dog's leash and ran on either side of her, scrambling upward over the slope behind them. In only a moment they were standing at the edge of the ravine, the familiar one in their own neighborhood. The mist was disappearing in the morning sun. Some distance away, Jeremy could see Mrs. Ramey's garden, with Mrs. Ramey in it. And when he looked back down the sloping bank, there was the clump of bushes that marked the fort. He shook his head to clear it, but none of his confusion went away.

"There's the fort," he said to Quinn. "At least I think so. Want to go back for the knife?" He hoped not.

"Huh-uh." Quinn kept staring down the way they had come.

"We can do it some other time," Jeremy said.

"Right." Quinn finally turned away. "Let's go to my house and watch cartoons."

"Right," echoed Jeremy. "We don't have to do any battles today, okay?"

Quinn nodded, and then they walked on in the kind of silence that comes from shared amazement.

Only Duchess seemed untroubled, licking and nudging and wagging as usual.

CHAPTER 5

❖ *Ulf*

It was all the talk in the royal household, and it went on for days. The queen had said this to the outlander girl, or that, or maybe another thing. And now that Prince Ar was too far away to offer his protection, this was the punishment the queen had decreed—or no, not exactly that, but worse. Gossip flew in the kitchen; dark stories raced along the chill corridors. All Ulf knew for sure was that he saw no sign of Gudrun for one day and then two. On the third, he resolved to talk to Old Berta, in spite of the deeper and deeper silence into which she had fallen since the wizard had gone away.

"The queen is in a rage," he said to the old woman that night as she sat with eyes fixed on the dim coals of their night's fire. "Gudrun the Fair would not agree to have the prince for her husband. Did you know that, Berta?" There was no response. "And after he left, some say, the queen ordered one of the watchmen to give her a beating." Ulf swallowed. He did not like to think this could be true.

"Others say the queen has locked her away forever. And maybe that is so, because I do not see her anymore." He noticed that Berta's head began to turn ever so slightly in his direction, and he hurried on. "But I have also heard that the queen has forced her to be a servant—sent her to work as a washerwoman where the stream comes to the river. And they say it is long days she must spend there, longer even than the cook requires of me." Ulf stopped for breath; he was not accustomed to long speeches.

"Could we—" He stopped again. The old woman was frowning; her eyes had gone back to the fire. He sighed. Finding words was an effort. He would rather be silent, like Old Berta. And yet he felt a tie to Gudrun that urged him on. After all, they were both outlanders. And they shared the secret of the dog. Ulf took heart and started over.

"Could we— I mean, could *I* help her in some way? You are as wise as the wizard, aren't you, Berta? Can you tell me how to help her?"

No sound disturbed the quiet of the hut, not even a whisper from the coals on the hearth. Finally, Old Berta turned to him and showed him a hint of her crooked smile. Yet she raised her shoulders and let them fall, shrugging off his questions.

After he lay down to sleep, Ulf heard her thin singing for the first time in many nights. Her voice was high and strange in his ears without Harket's deeper tones to balance it. Still, he took some comfort from it, and some hope.

Before the dawn, he was wakened by that same voice speaking his own name in his ear. "Ulf!" Old Berta waited until he sat up and stretched. "If you go now," she said, "between moon and sun, none will see you. And you will be there to greet her."

"Where?" He was suddenly full awake. "Where should I go?"

"She goes to the river before the light, and you will hear her before you see her, for she drags the queen's washing behind her in a great bundle." Berta gripped his arm. "Mind you are not too quick to speak," she said. "Wait until she is alone."

"What way should I take?" Ulf felt his teeth clattering softly, for which he blamed the cold. "How will I know the place?"

"Follow the path by the stream to its end. The way is easy."

"And when I find her, then what can I do?" He felt suddenly foolish. He had asked for help and received it, and now he did not know what to do with it. "Could you come with me, Berta?" The plea slipped out between his lips, much as he wanted to keep it in.

She began to shake her head before the words were

done. "Ah," she said, "you do seem young, but you still have to find your own way, lad. No one can do it for you." All she would give him was a bit to eat and a packet of salve. "For the poor girl's fingers," she said. "They will be raw as meat in all that cold water." And then she hustled him out into the dark.

Ulf was grateful that the mists were thin, nothing but narrow ribbons of a paler dark here and there along the water. He could scarcely see his feet, but he could look up and see the stars, and they gave him courage to make his way downstream. The path was familiar for only a little distance; thereafter he had to give it his full attention, feeling his way along. He heard the slow gurgle of the river before he came to it, and then he saw the dark shine of it and the flatness along the bank where there was no shelter. All at once the sky began to glow, taking the color of old silver and growing brighter by the moment. He hid himself among the trees along the path and waited, but not for long.

Gudrun came past him with halting steps, a ghostly figure dragging a huge bag behind her. Ulf wished that he could take the great leather strap that pulled against her shoulder as the bag bounced over roots and stones. But remembering Old Berta's warning, he did not allow himself to leave the cover of the trees. In a moment more he saw the guard, a great hulking man who moved along the path some distance behind. He stopped, watching, as

Gudrun reached the edge of the river. The guard shouted instructions to her with threats and curses that made Ulf cringe, but the girl stood looking out over the water as if no one spoke. Finally the man snarled a promise to return and took himself back the way they had come, past the place where Ulf still hid and then out of sight along the path.

For a moment more, Ulf waited. Now that he knew Gudrun to be so far above his own rank in life, he was more shy than ever about speaking to her. He was trying to decide by what title he should address her when his foot moved by mistake, snapping a dry branch.

"Who's there?" Gudrun cried, whirling to face the sound. "Who comes to taunt me today, so early?"

The boy came out into the path. "It is Ulf," he said, stepping forward to give her a better look. "You know I mean no harm."

He was close enough to hear the long breath that came out of her. "Ohhh," she said. "Ulf! The one who carries water. I had feared never to see a friendly face again."

Pleased but embarrassed, he ducked his head.

"Here." He reached inside his tunic and pulled out the packet Old Berta had given him. "The wizard's wife sends this to you." He swallowed a stammer and licked his lips. "For your fingers, she said."

Gudrun beamed as she rubbed a bit of the salve into her hands. "Take her my thanks," she said, "and also the warning."

"What warning?" There was no sun as yet, but the light was clear, and Ulf had seen the feeling that flashed in the girl's face.

"I told you once," she said, lowering her voice as if the trees might have ears of their own. "My brother will come for me, and there will be killing, and those who have befriended me must hide themselves. You must not be seen then, nor the wizard and his wife. You are as innocent as I, both of us stolen away and brought here against our will. And the old couple do not serve *her*, I am sure of it."

"Her?"

"The queen! That wicked Erlinda! She who tries to shame me with the lowliest of tasks, and then sends her women to jeer at me. I think she would have me beaten if she could be sure it would leave no mark."

Ulf chewed his lip. He could not tell which frightened him more—the thought of the queen or the sight of his gentle friend grown fierce as a thunderbolt.

"I thought the queen wanted you to marry Prince Ar," he said. "Why would she want to hurt you? Or shame you?" Then Ulf worried that he had said too much, for how should he have known the queen's wishes? But Gudrun seemed to see nothing amiss, and he began to think that her place in the royal household had been a mystery to him only.

"She is full of hate for me," the girl said, "because I

would not come here willingly. But I was already promised to the Prince of Zirn." Ulf nodded; he knew.

The anger in Gudrun's face gave way to sadness as she went on. "She only wanted me as Ar's wife in the hope that her grandchildren would be fair to look on. And now—" Gudrun turned away from Ulf to look at the river. "Now that I have refused him again and he has scolded her for the way she treated me, she treats me worse than ever. I have come between her and her son, she says. I have turned him against her, she says, and I am to pay for it. There is no imagining what will happen when the war troop comes again."

Ulf searched for some word of comfort to offer her. "Maybe the king—" he began, but Gudrun said "No!" with such sudden strength that he did not even finish the thought in his own mind.

"The king killed my father," the girl said in a voice gone flat. "When I was taken, my family pursued me, and my own father died at Ludwig's hand. And then Ludwig took me on a ship to an island high above the sea and there presented me to Armut. I was to be his son's prize, his share of plunder from that raid."

Ulf listened with a full heart, for he could remember the pain of his own journey to this land, if not its particulars.

"When I refused the prince that first time," Gudrun said, "Ludwig was too angry to speak." She was whispering now, so that Ulf had to move closer to hear her. "He grabbed my hair instead and pulled me to the edge of the cliff and would have thrown me into the sea."

She was silent for so long that Ulf thought she would say no more, and he burned to know. "What then?" he prodded. "What happened?"

"Prince Ar persuaded him to let me go. He said that if I lived, I might still one day be a willing bride."

"Oh." Ulf frowned. "Would Prince Ar not be a good husband?"

Gudrun made a sound that was half sob, half disgust. "For someone else, he might!" The spirit that had drained away as she talked returned to her voice. "Listen, young Ulf, and understand." She turned to him and put one hand on each of his shoulders. "Armut is comely and proud and even kind, sometimes, in spite of his parents' example. But Erik of Zirn is all those things and more. I have known him all my life and loved him for most of it, and I will be nobody's wife if not his."

Ulf nodded. He had listened, and he was trying to understand, but he knew even less of love than he knew of magic.

"You should go, little brother," she said. "Even now the cook will take you to task for being late, and I have more to do here than I would wish." She poked the giant leather bag with her toe and sighed.

"Mind you remember what I said about thanking the wizard's wife," she called softly as he left.

Ulf raised one arm and waved it, to reassure her. But now that he knew Gudrun's plight, he felt, more than ever, powerless to help her and forlorn about the future. He tried to hope for her sake that she would be rescued, but the prospect of the killing she had predicted lodged in his stomach and gnawed there like a twin to his ever-present hunger. It was just as painful to imagine a time when she might be gone, when he would be the only out-lander with bright hair in this place. He would be completely friendless, unless the dog would come again. And who knew what Harket might have done about the dog?

His head was churning so by the time he reached the scullery that he took little notice of the sound thumping the cook decided he had earned. What was it after all but a few new bruises to keep the old ones company? He gave his real attention that day to a feeling that grew stronger and stronger inside him. Whatever happened, he must not hide. He must find a way to stand beside the one who had called him little brother. If only he had the dog, Magic, he thought, together they might make sure no harm would come to Gudrun the Fair. And together, perhaps, they could go away with her to a place where there was no heavy-fisted cook nor any thought of danger for golden dogs.

❖ *Jeremy*

On Sunday, Jeremy's mother made cinnamon rolls and scrambled eggs and fruit salad for brunch. She played card games with his little brother and read him the comics. She didn't say one word to his father about the volume control for the television, which went full blast all that rainy afternoon, from one football game to another and back again. She even brushed Duchess, with no more than a frown for the burrs that still clung to the long hair on the dog's underside.

Jeremy knew without being told that his mother was getting along well now with her project. When she went into her study after supper, he thought it was safe to follow her, to stretch out on the old brown couch with a book and wait for a chance to talk to her. He had questions, but he was not sure how to ask them, and so he was glad that his mother spoke first.

"Jeremy, why don't you read this thing I'm working on? I finally figured out most of my problems with the translation, and I've read every other version I could find, so I'm pretty far along with my own. You might be interested this time."

"That's okay, Mom. Thanks anyway." In Jeremy's estimation, all the documents his mother changed from one language to another were completely and totally boring.

"Well, let me know if you change your mind. This one's really a story, not some dry old business paper."

"Honest, Mom, no time." Jeremy held up the copy of *Old Yeller* that his teacher had given him. "I have to read this for school." He pretended to focus on the print, but his mother kept watching him.

"You've been glum all day," she said. "And you haven't even mentioned Quinn's name, not once. What's wrong, Jeremy?"

"Nothing." Nothing he could talk about anyway. But he felt a little better just because his mother had asked, and he didn't want her to lose herself in her work now, to go away from him inside her head.

"Well," he went on, "nothing much. I've just been wondering about stuff."

"Such as?" She smiled at him over the untidy pile of papers on her work table.

He took a breath. "Like . . . like, can you be wide awake and still be dreaming? Could that ever happen?"

"Honestly, Jeremy," his mother said, which wasn't an answer at all. But now that he had started, he couldn't stop.

"And could two people have the exact same dream at the same time? People who were awake, I mean?"

"Are you serious, Jeremy?" She shook her head slowly, in wonderment. "I'd be glum, too, if I spent my time thinking about things like that."

He sat straight and tried to make himself as believable as possible. "Okay," he said, "so, would it be, like, legal to ride a horse in the ravine? Could a person put on an old-time costume and ride right down the middle of the stream?" He could hear what an odd question it was, and he wished right away that he could take it back.

His mother stared at him. "I think you've had a dream, all right," she said, swiveling her chair to face the computer. "I should have guessed this had something to do with the ravine." *Chinnng!* Her monitor began to glow.

"I don't know which thing to worry about most," she went on, picking at the keyboard until Jeremy saw lines of print flash on the screen. "First it's you and Quinn with all those war games on your mind, nothing but soldiers and weapons and awful stuff. And now you're obsessed with the ravine. Don't think I didn't know that you've been down there, Jeremy. Maybe you did see some misguided soul on a horse. Who knows? It doesn't seem to matter how much I warn you about the dangers—"

"But Mom—" Jeremy said. He wanted to tell her that it had been almost thirty-six hours since he had even touched an ancient warrior. He wanted to tell her that he thought he wouldn't go back into the ravine, not ever, or at least not until he was a grandfather or something. He wanted to tell her that maybe she should stay out of the ravine, too, because such a weird thing had happened there. But Jeremy's mother was not in a listening mood.

"I have to tell you, Jeremy," she said, "that there were two break-ins in the neighborhood last week, both of them along the ravine and one in broad daylight. It wasn't anything big, I guess, but you just don't understand how careful you need to be."

Jeremy sighed. "Yes, I do," he said. If only she knew.

His mother turned around to look at him. "Max DaSilva is so concerned about it that he's thinking about getting new locks put in—deadbolts."

"Quinn's dad?" Jeremy frowned, thinking it was true that Mr. DaSilva had always been strict about locking the doors.

"I don't blame him," Jeremy's mother said, "with that valuable collection in the house. He probably should just put it in a museum."

"What collection?" Jeremy began to picture the rooms in the DaSilva house, one by one, checking for items a thief might want.

"You must have seen it. There are things from all over the world that Quinn's great-grandfather brought home from his travels."

Jeremy began to feel so weak that he had to hold on to the arm of the couch. Quinn's knife might be worth a lot of money. "Yeah," he said, trying to sound casual. "But I haven't exactly seen it. Quinn's dad keeps it locked up in that big black box."

Jeremy's mother smiled. "That's an ebony chest," she said, "and a work of art in itself, and maybe we should just forget this whole discussion. You're pale as you can be all of a sudden."

"I'm okay," he said, but he didn't quite trust his voice.

"I wasn't trying to frighten you, Jeremy." His mother got up and came to him, laying the back of her hand against his forehead. "You aren't catching something, are you?"

"I'm okay," he repeated, but it was an automatic answer, not a real one. He blinked, trying to clear away the image of Quinn's very valuable dagger wrapped in a painted T-shirt and buried under a rock. In the ravine.

His mother stepped back, but he could tell by the way she kept looking at him that she was trying to puzzle him out, as if he were one of her projects that needed translation.

"You'll use good judgment about the ravine, won't you, Jeremy?"

He nodded.

"You'll stay out of there?"

"Honest, Mom, I'd only go into the ravine if I just had to." That was the truth, Jeremy thought ruefully. "If it was a real emergency, I mean." The trouble was, he was afraid that recovering the dagger qualified as a real emergency. He didn't want to lie to his mother, but somehow the whole truth seemed too complicated now to explain. He stood up. "I didn't mean to bother you, Mom," he said. "I'll go read in my room."

"It's all right, Jeremy, really. I'm almost done with the

first draft, and then I'll just have the polishing left to do." Some of the worry lines in his mother's forehead smoothed themselves out. "I'm not sure that everything's right, even now, but it's quite a story, any way you look at it." She was smiling. "There's a cruel queen and a captive princess, and a prince who comes to her rescue—actually, *two* princes."

"Hnh," said Jeremy. He was definitely not interested in captive princesses, although he thought the part that Quinn had found on that piece of scrap paper about kings who fought to the death might be worth reading someday. What he was really thinking was how he needed to talk to Quinn. They had a rescue operation of their own to plan, whether they wanted to or not.

"And then there's a huge battle, Jeremy, with plenty of blood and gore even for you and Quinn."

"Cool," he said, but he wasn't really listening. He was wondering how soon Quinn would want to make another try to recover the knife. They had started to talk about it yesterday, but they couldn't decide how dangerous it might be. Quinn's father had taken him away on an errand, and by the time they came back, Quinn had a sore throat and couldn't play anymore. Jeremy wished they could have settled it, talked it out. Today, when he called, he kept getting the answering machine.

"You haven't heard a word I've been saying," his mother said.

"I have, too." He made his mouth smile at her. "It sounds great, Mom."

She shook her head and chuckled. "Why don't you just go do your reading wherever you want," she said. "Or better yet, go check on Austin and find out why he's been so quiet for so long."

Jeremy didn't want to check on Austin, but he found him without meaning to. When he opened his own bedroom door, there was Austin right in the middle of his bed. Duchess was stretched out beside him amid a jumble of ancient warriors and their boxes.

"Hey!" Jeremy protested. "What do you think you're doing?" Jeremy's room was supposed to be off-limits to his little brother. And his model soldiers were supposed to be completely and absolutely untouchable.

"Look!" Austin said. His face was radiant with pleasure. "Look at this one, Jeremy!"

Jeremy bit his lip. It was a tiny warrior on horseback that Austin held out to him, a warrior with royal trappings, the very image of the horseman in the ravine. A shiver passed over him, a tiny rattle of fear that made him irritated and almost ashamed. He felt like hitting something. Austin deserved a good smack for messing with his things, Jeremy thought. He raised his hand, but somehow it came down easy, no more than a pat on the bright red target that was the back of Austin's T-shirt. He felt an unexpected rush of protective feeling. Austin was trouble, all right, but he was still little. He was okay for a little guy. Duchess thumped her tail against the bedspread. Jeremy began to feel a bit better, one more step away from all that strangeness on Saturday morning.

"Okay, troops," he said, handing Austin a box. "Time to clean up here." Maybe, somehow, things would work out.

CHAPTER 6

Ulf

There came a day soon when the wind blew cold, bringing with it waves of rain. Ulf was put to new tasks in such weather—scrubbing and cleaning, or helping to tend the kitchen fire. He coveted this last for its warmth, but he dreaded it, too, for he never knew when the wood gatherers might come with new fuel for the huge storage box in the corner of the room.

He crouched warily by the hearth that day, keeping the smoky blaze alive and turning to treat both sides of his body to the heat of it. For some time no one passed by the fire, not even the cook, and there were no sounds but the hiss of hot wood and the slow bubble of soup. In the quiet, Ulf let down his guard. He fell to thinking about the dog and about the wizard, who was absent even yet, and about Gudrun the Fair. He wondered if her royal brother might be at this very moment leading his men through the rain to her rescue. On the next clear day, he vowed to himself, he would slip away and see how she fared.

Ulf was drowsy now and completely warm, and his mind was no longer focused on tending the fire. He was very near to dreaming, and so he did not at first take notice of the footsteps that approached, or hear the voices. One moment he was as comfortable as a boy could be, and then came a blow that sent him tumbling into the hot rim of ash at the front of the fire. He cried out in surprise and pain.

Puli and another boy stood over him, laughing and jeering. "Clumsy outlander!" "Look at him!"

Ulf managed to roll away from the coals and get to his knees. With stinging hands, he brushed at the ashes that clung to him. "You pushed me!" he said in disgust. Burns were among the worst of wounds, slow to heal, often deadly. "Why should you put me in the fire?" he cried as he stood to face the others, anger rising up in him.

Puli was ready to use his fist for an answer, but the cook came lumbering in from the scullery, cursing days of rain and shouting for them to be quiet. He began to rant at all three of them, and Ulf thought his tirade might have gone on until mealtime if there had not been a sharp little sound, a hand clap, to stop it. All of them looked at once to the kitchen's wide-arched entrance. There stood Queen Erlinda, her hands still pressed together. It seemed to Ulf that her presence came across the warm room like an icy draft, chilling everything.

"Who is to blame for this brawl?" She spoke slowly, without raising her voice. Ulf trembled, not daring to tell her, but Puli and the other boy began to point at him. He shook his head, trying to stammer a denial.

"Silence!" The queen's eyes traveled from his face to the cook's and came to rest on the wood gatherers. "I saw you," she said, "and you should be punished. But your kinsmen serve me well, and for their sakes I give you only a warning,"

For a moment, Ulf thought she was finished; she seemed about to turn and walk away. But then the queen smiled unpleasantly and nodded at Puli. "The next time you two cause a disturbance," she said, "I will send you down to the river with the outlander girl, our most precious princess." Ulf shuddered at the mockery in her voice.

"The cook will be able to find some washing for you to do," the queen continued, "and you can do it every single day, as she does, whatever the weather." She laughed, and the sound of it was ugly in Ulf's ears.

One of the watchmen came up the corridor then, and she turned and stepped into the shadows to speak to him.

"*Washing!*" whispered the boy who stood with Puli, and

the crowd of kitchen lads who had gathered so quietly now snickered behind their hands. The very thought of a wood gatherer doing women's work was beyond their imagining. Puli turned a look of blazing hatred toward Ulf, but Ulf paid him little attention. His thoughts had flown to Gudrun. Even today, in the wind and the rain and the cold, she must have been taken to the river.

While the cook berated all his boys in a lower voice, Ulf breathed slowly, trying to think. Gudrun was every day at the river, and the queen had threatened to send Puli there also. If only he could be punished like that himself, Ulf thought, he would be able to watch over his friend, to stand with her. But what could he say or do that would earn the desired result? If he overstepped his bounds too far, the queen might— He did not go on to the end of that thought, for he knew well enough that Queen Erlinda held the power of life and death for all of her household when the king was away.

Ulf was thinking so hard that it took some time for him to realize that everyone in the kitchen had grown quiet again, even the cook. The only voices now came from the shadows outside the archway, where he could hear the queen's agitated questions and the watchman's hesitant replies.

"When was it they returned?"

"Just now. Just now, my queen."

"And you saw them yourself? And they did not have it with them?"

"I—I talked to the men of the guard with my own mouth, mistress, but the old man had gone on. Empty-handed, so they said."

"He is more fool than wizard, I would say." The queen's tone was full of contempt.

Ulf, who was just beginning to understand the conversation, fastened on the word *wizard* and held his breath. Where was Harket now? Had he come home?

"And they found no sign of the creature in all this land, my queen. They searched from the upper reach of the forest to the far side of the river." The watchman lowered his voice as the kitchen boys strained to hear. "I tell you, mistress, the guards do not think there is such a beast. There is no golden wolf, they say."

"There *is*!" The queen screamed out the words. "There *is* a golden wolf! Some of my own women saw it!"

Ulf stared down at the hearth as he listened. He could not see the eyes of the others come to rest on him, yet he felt their gaze as surely as if they had touched him.

"There is a golden wolf," Erlinda cried, "and I shall have it! If I cannot have it in a cage to admire, then I shall have its fur to wear about my neck! Tell them to keep up the hunt!"

Horror rose up in Ulf's throat. Its fur, she had said. *Its fur!* His feet moved before any thought told them to do it, carrying him faster than he knew he could move, under the kitchen arch and toward the voices. "No!" he shouted. "No! *No!* It's only a dog!" He flung himself toward the queen, and by then he was sobbing.

The watchman's big hand caught and held him by the neck while the queen screeched and squawked and rubbed at the smudge Ulf's sooty fingers had left on her gown. "Filthy child!" she cried. "This filthy child dared to touch the queen! Take him out and—" Ulf never knew what sentence she had started to pronounce, but she stopped in the midst of it and looked at him more closely.

"This is the one to go to the river," she said smugly. "It will keep him out of my sight, and if an outlander falls in— well, what's the loss?"

Ulf's tears disappeared. His vision was clear enough to see the cook scowling at such a waste of a water carrier and the boys all trying to hide their laughter. It was all he could do to keep from laughing himself, in delight at this outcome, although the watchman's grip on his neck was reason enough to be silent.

"Shall I take him there now, my queen?" The man gave Ulf a shake as if to prove that he had control of this situation, in spite of his powerlessness in the matter of the golden wolf.

"Good-bye, wizard's boy," called someone in the kitchen.

The queen brushed at her skirt again. "Begone!" she said. "Take him, and waste no time about it!" The glance that passed across Ulf's face was sharp and menacing as a blade.

She nodded to the watchman, and in less than a moment Ulf was swept out of the shelter of the keep into the pounding rain. For someone so suddenly cold and wet, he was very happy. He had escaped the queen's gaze, and he was on his way to be with Gudrun.

"Can you find your own way from here, boy?" the watchman asked as they came out of the forest and into the ravine. "I don't care to live like the fishes today."

Ulf nodded.

The man seized his shoulder. "Do you know what will happen if you aren't there with her when her guard comes to bring her in?"

Ulf nodded again. He would rather pretend to know than have the explanation, he thought.

"Your chances wouldn't be any better than that wolf's, I tell you." The watchman released his grip. "Whatever the queen sets her mind on, she gets," he whispered, "and you best not forget that. Now go on! Run!"

Ulf ran, slipping on wet rock and sliding in mud, catching at branches to keep from falling into the swollen stream. Magic was no ordinary dog, he told himself. If she had not let Harket see her, she would not let the queen's men find her now. He thought of her with longing, how he had dreamed the two of them might leave this place with Gudrun some day. But now was a dangerous time. "Hide well, my Magic," he sang softly, watching his feet. "Magic, hide well." And then he looked up and there she was, a little way downstream, just coming off the high path onto the bank.

⁂ *Jeremy*

Jeremy could not believe his rotten luck. Number one, it wasn't Friday. It had been Thursday all day, wet and dreary since breakfast. Number two, Quinn really did have a sore throat. He had been sick all week, no visitors allowed. The one time Jeremy had gotten him on the phone, Quinn could only croak a few words. And to make matters worse, today one of Austin's friends from day care had come home with him to stay until dinnertime. At first the two of them wore their sweatshirts and played on the porch, but little by little they brought all of Austin's toy cars and trucks into the family room, complete with sound effects— revving motors, wailing sirens, beeping horns.

"Hey, Austin! Tyler! Can't you guys be quieter?" Jeremy had spread his homework out on one end of the kitchen island and was staring at a whole page of fractions. He thought his mother would take the hint and make the little boys calm down, but she just smiled and went on making meatballs.

"Maybe you can do your homework after dinner," she said.

The noise level rose. Austin's friend sat down in a big yellow dump truck and began to scoot across the carpet toward Duchess, who got up and trotted away.

"Cowboys!" yelled Austin. "Get the cow!" And in a moment they were both chasing after the dog, who began to bark nonstop in accompaniment to their gleeful screeching.

"All right," Jeremy's mother said. "I give up. Take the dog for a walk, Jeremy. Please."

"Mom!" he said. "It's still raining."

"You can wear your poncho."

"She'll get all wet and smelly!"

"So don't forget to towel her off when you get home."

He closed his math book with a thump, but he didn't offer any more complaints. Being out in the rain with Duchess wouldn't be all that bad compared to the chaos inside.

When he got the dog's harness, Austin and Tyler clamored to go, too, but his mother told them absolutely not. "You be careful, Jeremy," she said.

He was glad to escape. The rain had slowed to a heavy drizzle. He liked the sound of it on the poncho that covered his head, although he didn't like the way the plastic stuck out, stiff and green, around his cheeks. Duchess was a slow traveler on wet days, and he had to creep along behind her, stopping and starting as she sniffed and moved on, trying to keep her out of the mud. They made their way up the winding street and around the middle-school ball field, crossed the bridge over the ravine, and continued on Sycamore Heights. The street and the sidewalks were empty. There was nothing but the rain, and the dog, and all those things he had to think about. His math homework wasn't even close to the top of the list.

He had stewed all week about what had happened in the ravine on Saturday, trying to figure it out. He worried, too, about the dagger that must be one of the relics Quinn's great-grandfather had collected. If it was as valuable as his mother thought, he and Quinn would have to go after it for sure. But what if they ended up in that other place again? He wished Quinn hadn't gotten sick. He needed to talk to him, to find out if he had any ideas.

Duchess tugged against her harness, pulling him on around the corner to Morning Street. Jeremy frowned. He hadn't been on this edge of the ravine since that foggy day when Duchess had run away from Austin. She didn't like her harness very well, but it did make her easier to handle, he had to admit.

He remembered how she had come charging down

toward the fort on Saturday, pulling Quinn along behind. A smile crept across his face. He almost wished he had a video of that, of Quinn bouncing down the hill, except that it would always remind him of the fright that came afterward. He stood waiting while Duchess gave her full attention to the roots of a tree, and his head replayed Saturday's scene over and over. First he was there at the fort in the ravine, and then Duchess and Quinn came hurtling down the hill. And then the fort suddenly wasn't there, but a mountain *was*, and the stream was loud, and the ancient warrior came on horseback. . . . It wasn't the same ravine, he was sure. But after that, he and Quinn had followed Duchess up the slope, and they were home again, without any trouble at all. It was almost as if the dog had taken them somewhere far away, years away, and brought them back again. Jeremy rubbed his wet forehead and thought of what Ms. Hernandez had been telling them in school: If you wanted to find out whether something was true, you had to experiment, test it out. He swallowed hard.

"Duchess!" The dog turned her head and looked at him.

"I've got an idea," Jeremy said, "but you really have to cooperate, okay?" He led her away from the street and around some scraggly bushes with wet brown leaves to the very edge of the ravine. "I'm going to go down there to that rock, see? It's only a couple of steps, really, but you have to stay here while I do it. Okay, girl?" He stroked the damp fur between her ears. Then he secured the end of her leash by putting a piece of deadwood through the loop and wedging the limb among the lower branches of one of the bushes.

"Sit!" he told her, and she sat in the dripping grass beside the bush, whimpering once. "I'll be right back," he promised.

Jeremy went to the edge of the bank and looked over. He made himself memorize the location of the landmarks on the hill. Straight ahead was the rock, a big one with a flat top. To the right were some bare bushes and four trees with a few orange-gold leaves still clinging to their branches. On the left, a low stone fence, old and crumbling, wound for a little way down the hill before it disappeared. Far below, the road and the stream, visible now from the day's rain, meandered side by side through the ravine.

Jeremy took a deep breath. "I'll be right back," he said again to the dog. He wiped a wet hand over his wet face and adjusted his poncho to keep the water away from his neck. He put one foot onto the slippery hillside, resting a hand on the old stone fence for balance. If he didn't hurry, he thought, he might lose his nerve.

Two more careful steps, and then another, and he was standing on the same rock he had seen from the edge of the ravine. He smiled. No mountain. Nothing seemed new or unfamiliar. Duchess, just out of his sight, began to bark.

"Just a minute, now," he called to her, but he took his time looking around. There were the trees with their wet golden leaves; there were the road and the stream. Nothing had changed. "Okay, Duchess!" he called, hurrying back up to the top. "Now for you!"

She twisted and turned, trying to lick him, while he disentangled her leash from the bush. "We'll go down together this time," he said, "but only a step or two, just in case." His sensible side shouted at him that he shouldn't do this part, but how else would he know? He put his hand through the loop at the end of the leash and then wrapped it three times around his wrist for good measure.

"Good dog," he said, "come on," but she needed no encouragement. It was Jeremy whose feet wanted to go backward at the ravine's edge. Duchess shook herself, spraying water on all sides, and then she stepped down onto the bank. When Jeremy saw her tail begin to move, he took a deep breath and followed.

Suddenly, it was pouring, and because the rain made it hard to see, it took him a moment to get his bearings. When he did, he was afraid his heart might stop. There was no fence, no flat rock. A mountain wrapped in a shawl of mist loomed to one side. At the bottom of the ravine was a stream running so swift and full in the rain that it covered most of the path beside it.

His experiment had worked, but he felt more like calling for help than celebrating his success. He wished he had never thought of it. He wished Quinn was with him. He wished his dog would slow down on the slippery hillside.

"Duchess, stay!" he said as sharply as his failing breath would allow. And just as he spoke, there came a soft, insistent whistle from below. She ignored his command and pulled harder against her harness.

"Magic! Maaa-gic!"

Jeremy heard the voice and saw who spoke all in one moment. It was a boy, coming toward him up the slope in garments so wet and shapeless that Jeremy couldn't tell what they were. But he was too slight and bedraggled to seem much of a threat, and Jeremy's racing heart began to slow.

The boy saw him, Jeremy knew, because he stopped abruptly some way off, and the two of them looked at each other through the rain. Jeremy's grip on the dog's leash was so tight the edges hurt his hands; he didn't trust the way Duchess was wagging and leaning forward, being so friendly.

Jeremy wondered if he should speak, if he should ask this boy who he was. But his caution overcame his curiosity, and all he did was raise his free hand in greeting. Then, suddenly, he was overwhelmed by the strangeness of it all.

"Come on, Duchess!" he whispered, and gave her so firm

a yank that she had to turn and follow his frantic steps upward. The boy below shouted after him, but Jeremy didn't stop, and in a moment he and the dog were at the edge of the ravine, scrambling onto level ground with a clear view of Morning Street. Yes! he thought, Safe! He looked back from the top. There was the rock, there was the old stone wall. He hurried Duchess to the sidewalk, where he slowed down, grateful for drizzle in place of downpour. He was out of breath, exhausted. He was amazed at himself, how incredibly brave he had been. And he marveled at Duchess.

"You're something, all right," he whispered to her. "When you go down into the ravine, look what happens!" He shook his head in bewilderment. "Just wait till I tell Quinn!" Maybe Quinn wouldn't even believe it, especially the part about the boy.

But in the midst of his excitement, it occurred to Jeremy that it might be dangerous to have a magical dog—or to be one. He frowned and urged Duchess to walk faster as they headed home. The ravine was way too weird, worse than his mother thought by far. Maybe he and Quinn would be lucky enough to get the knife back safely, and then they could stay out of the ravine forever.

CHAPTER 7

❖ Ulf

The wizard had come home from the hunt. Ulf knew it as
soon as he stepped onto the muddy doorpath and saw the
smoke rising above the battered roof. Old Berta never
stoked the fire high for herself, or for Ulf. And this night
there was even the scent of roasting fowl on the still-damp
air. He tried to hurry, but his body was tired and slow. Not
even one whole day had he been at the river with Gudrun
the Fair, and he knew already that the time would be
hard—hard and hungry. Now he breathed deeply, wrin-
kling his nose, hoping for a tidbit of crispy skin or a bite of
meat. It was the prospect of food and warmth that drew
him up the path, for the thought of meeting with the wizard made his steps falter. There would be too many questions, too many things to tell.

And so he was surprised, and relieved, that Harket greeted him in silence. The old man nodded from his seat by the fire and turned his eyes back to the flames while Ulf gobbled the drumstick Berta had saved for him. When he had swallowed the last morsel, he began to chew on the bone, taking his time, putting off the moment that must come. But at last Ulf could not bear the waiting; he was unnerved by the press of things unspoken in that small, warm room.

"Harket, sir," he began, "I—I thank you for bringing no harm to the dog."

The wizard turned in his seat to look at him. "And how can you be so sure of that, boy?" His voice was hushed and deep, like faraway thunder.

"Because I saw her this day, on the high bank, in the rain." Ulf paused. These words came easily; he had told this much to Gudrun at the washing stone. If only that were the end of it. But the wizard stared into his face as if he could see behind Ulf's eyes.

"Tell it all," he said.

Ulf had to swallow. "She was on a tether."

The wizard was perfectly still, listening.

"It was not to tie her," Ulf said sadly. "Someone held it, to walk with her."

A sharp sound of dismay came from the end of the bench where Old Berta sat. "I knew it!" she whispered. "They never come alone!"

The wizard held up his hand to her for silence. "Tell us more," he said to Ulf, and his voice was urgent now. "You must tell everything. Who was it that walked with the dog?" It seemed to Ulf that Harket's eyes sparked as bright as the fire.

"It was a boy, I think," he said softly. "But he was . . . an outlander." The word sounded strange out of his own mouth. He thought of the way the dog had followed her companion up over the edge of the ravine and out of sight, on a tether, but without complaint. Envy filled Ulf's heart. "Maybe it could have been a troll," he said. "He wore a green cloak that shone like a fish's belly. No one has a cloak that shines in the rain, not even Prince Ar."

Harket blinked, and for an instant Ulf thought the questions were finished. But they were not. "Think!" the wizard demanded of Ulf. "Think if you ever saw that boy-creature before."

"I—I might have." He wished that he could look away from the old man's eyes, but they held him despite the dim light and the table between them. "On the first day I saw the dog," he said, "I thought there were three of them— three of something—up on the high path. The mists were thick that day." He stammered out his excuses. "I—I was not sure if my eyes tricked me. And then I didn't see them again." And I wanted to forget about them, he added silently.

Harket turned to his wife. "It is as I feared," he said. His voice was low and somber. "A slip. An entrapment."

Old Berta nodded. Her lips were set in a thin, straight line. "Dangerous business," she whispered.

"But how can they be a danger?" Ulf looked from the wizard to his wife and back again. "The one yesterday was not that much bigger than I am. And he did not act like an enemy. He even raised his hand to greet me."

Harket arched one eyebrow. "And you—?"

"I shouted at him that he should hide the dog because the queen wants to put her in a cage, or"—it was all Ulf could do to keep his voice from shaking—"or to wear her beautiful fur. I could not tell if he heard me, but he ran and took the dog with him."

The wizard frowned. "Where did they go?"

"Up. After they got to the high path, I couldn't see them anymore."

Harket nodded. "Yes," he said. "That would be the way." The old man beckoned Ulf to leave his bench and sit by the hearth. "Come closer, boy," he said. "Come to the fire and stay warm while you tell me what other secrets you have been keeping."

And so Ulf warmed himself as the fire sputtered, and the heat loosened his tongue, and the wizard's unexpected kindness gave him courage. He poured out all he knew about the dog, how it had saved him from Puli and been mistaken for a wolf. He spoke of Prince Ar and Gudrun and the queen's punishments. At each new detail, Harket nodded but showed no sign of surprise, although Berta mumbled darkly into the folds of her shawl. Ulf talked on, pausing only to sip the red herb tea that she brought for all three of them.

"And Gudrun says I am to warn you that her brother will come to rescue her, and there will be bloodshed." Ulf usually trembled when he thought of this, but it felt much safer, somehow, to be telling the wizard, who might know what to do. "She says those who have been kind to her should go into hiding then, because the queen's men will count them among the enemy." He shook his head. "But I don't want to hide. I want to stand with Gudrun and protect her." Color rose in his face when he said it, for he knew a boy of his size would be of little use, and of no use at all without a weapon.

"I could go away with her to her own land," he continued. "I would like to serve Gudrun instead of this queen. And I would take that dog if I had it, because then it wouldn't be any more trouble to you here and it would be out of the queen's reach—" Ulf saw Harket and his wife exchange a glance, and he realized that he had said more than he intended. He had told what he hoped as well as what he knew. He closed his mouth and stared at the glowing coals.

For a long time, no one spoke. An owl hooted nearby, and a gust of wind rattled through bare branches. Old Berta drained her cup. "The ice is not far off," she said. "Men do not go to battle when the ice comes. The brother will winter in his own keep. Even Ludwig will have turned for home by now."

Ulf caught his breath. What if Gudrun's brother came anyway, and what if he arrived at the same time as Ludwig's war troop? What if there would be such a terrible melee that Gudrun had no chance to escape? And what if the dog should come and be caught in it? Or never come again at all? He shook his head to clear it of such thoughts.

"Ulf," said Harket, "there are things that you must know about the dog."

"What things?" He looked up into the old man's face.

The wizard bent forward in his seat, closer to Ulf's ear. "I did see the creature. It is not dangerous in the way of a wolf. There is no viciousness in her. She is a fine dog, quite a beauty."

Ulf's cheeks widened in a huge smile at Harket's praise, but his moment of good cheer faded as the wizard went on.

"Yet she is a threat to us, make no mistake. She does not belong here, boy. Not here, nor in the girl's homeland." The wizard whispered now, putting his mouth against Ulf's ear, as if no part of his message dare be lost. "The dog is from a time that is not our own," Harket said, "and from a place where we would not be welcome."

Old Berta made the sign against evil and began to sing under her breath, a thin keening that brought Ulf no comfort.

"The dog ties us to that other place," the wizard said, "and to its people and to their ways. In all this land and the lands beyond, we have no power, no magic, to match theirs. If we are to finish the lives we have started, if we are to come to our own natural end, we must send the dog and all who travel with her back to their own realm to stay."

Ulf did not understand it all, but the last part, sending the dog away, that was clear. He put his head in his hands— partly to stop it from spinning, partly to hide his horrified expression. "She cannot be a wicked spirit," he protested, in a voice gone weak. "She is real, Harket, I know it! I have felt her breath on my face." He bit his lip, remembering.

The wizard glanced toward the hearth, where only one log glowed now among the embers. "Yes, boy," he said. "She is real, both in our world and in her own, but it is only by a slip, a happenstance. Something here called her to us—all unknowing, I would suppose. It might have been you."

"But—but she just appeared," Ulf said. Somewhere in his memory there floated the sound of his own whistle, calling her down into the ravine, and the echo of his own voice this very day, shouting through the rain the name he had given her: "Magic! Magic!" He opened his mouth to explain, but no words came.

"No matter," the wizard said, shaking his head and turn-ing now to the remains of the fire. "A lonely child in great need of a companion—that in itself could be enough for a slip. But it does not explain why that other world stays so near to ours, why the dog can come back again and again. Once is a slip, boy. Many times is an entrapment."

Ulf shivered at the sound of it, and Berta finally stopped her crooning. "Enough," she murmured to her husband, getting up to tend the fire. And to Ulf she said, "Go wrap up, boy. Sleep." The word was as good as a charm, and he knew nothing until the dark of morning.

✤ *Jeremy*

Jeremy pushed his spaghetti around on his plate. He didn't feel like eating. He was too breathless, somehow, for all that chewing and swallowing. All the energy he had left was already in use, up in his brain, where thoughts chased after one another like little kids on a playground. He just had to talk to Quinn, sore throat or no sore throat. They had plans to make. He went over the steps in his head for the umpteenth time. They would make sure Duchess was locked in the house; they would go to the fort and dig up Quinn's knife; they would return it to where Quinn's father thought it belonged. Then they would stay out of the ravine forever, and everything would be back to normal.

Maybe. Jeremy tried hard to believe it, but the effort made him sigh.

"Why aren't you eating, Jeremy?" His mother was looking at him with real concern—spaghetti was his favorite meal, after all—and in that instant, he almost told her. He almost blurted out to everyone how you could end up somewhere very old and far away if you went over the edge of the ravine with Duchess. But he stopped himself. Who would believe it? There wasn't one logical thing about it. What if somehow he had just imagined it, or had a hallucination or something? And he wasn't supposed to be in the ravine anyway.

"Eat up, Jeremy," his father said. Mr. Ervin sent a warning look across the table to both his sons. Austin was picking mushrooms out of his sauce and putting them under the rim of his plate, saying, "Uck, uck," under his breath. Jeremy thought it was a wonder that dinnertime could go on just as always when he had so much to worry about.

"You've been moping around for almost a whole week," his mother said to him. "Something must be wrong with you. Maybe you're getting Quinn's sore throat."

"No, Mom," he said. "Honest I'm not. Look—I ate all my salad already. Can't I be excused? I've got all those fractions to do."

She made a face but waved him away. "I'll save your dinner," she said, "just in case."

Jeremy scooped up his backpack and hurried up the

stairs, Duchess at his heels. If he was quick enough, he thought, he could call Quinn from the phone in his parents' bedroom before they finished eating. He picked up the handset, sank down into the thick rug beside the bed, and punched in the familiar numbers. The dog flopped herself down at his side. He closed his eyes and willed Quinn himself to answer, but it was Richelle.

"Let me talk to Quinn, okay, Richelle?" He hoped he didn't sound as impatient as he felt. Richelle could be a problem if she thought anything was going on.

"Is that you, Jeremy? Don't you know that Quinn's still sick? He's in bed, for heaven's sake. I'm not allowed to bother him."

Jeremy's breath caught for a moment in his throat. "Wouldn't he feel better, don't you think, if he had a chance to talk to his best friend?"

"Jeremy!" Richelle's laugh trilled out of the phone into his ear. "You are so cute sometimes!"

He cringed. When Richelle talked like that, he always wanted to throw up. "So can I talk to him?" he said.

"Of course not." He could hear Richelle's CD player in the background.

"When can I?"

"I don't know, Jeremy. He's had a really high fever. It might be days."

"Unnh." He put one hand over the mouthpiece to muffle his groan.

"And anyway, my dad is afraid you two have been going down into the ravine, and he's really hot about it."

Jeremy groaned again. He imagined the dagger and its scabbard stuck in the ravine forever, its blade heavy with rust, the leather damaged by mold.

"He says you're both due for a DaSilva debriefing."

"Oh, great," Jeremy said. Beside him, Duchess slept and dreamed, nose twitching, paws quivering.

He was ready to hang up, but Richelle was still talking. "You know why he's upset, don't you, Jeremy? It's because the ravine is dangerous now."

His hand gripped the telephone like a lifeline. "Who says?"

"Everybody, silly. There's been a prowler this last week or two all along the top bank. He doesn't even wait until night to come and snoop around."

Jeremy had to bite his tongue to keep the questions back. Did the prowler wear a costume? Was he riding a horse? Or was it just a boy? What he finally asked was, "Did anyone really see him?"

"Not until the other day," Richelle said. "And then Mrs. Ramey went out to sweep the leaves off her back terrace, and she saw him standing on tiptoe looking in one of the kitchen windows. It was an old gray-haired guy in a long coat, and he was carrying a great big stick, like a club or something."

Jeremy swallowed. "What did she do?"

"Screamed," Richelle said, in a tone that meant Jeremy should have figured that out for himself. "And she ran in and called nine-one-one, but by the time the cops got there, he had disappeared without a trace."

"Wow." Jeremy struggled to place this new image among the other surprises the ravine had offered.

"I have to go now, Jeremy," Richelle said. "I've got another call. Bye." The connection clicked off. He stared at the silent telephone and tried to think. When he finally moved to return it to its base on his mother's nightstand, he felt clumsy and thick. By accident, his hand brushed against a neat stack of paper on the corner of the stand, and it started to slide over the edge. When he tried to catch it, pages went swirling this way and that to the floor. Duchess, roused by the flurry, sniffed at the ones that had skimmed her fur, shook herself, and stalked out of the room.

For a moment, Jeremy considered leaving the mess where it lay, but then he took a deep breath and got down on his knees to pick up and sort. DRAFT was printed out at the top of every page, followed by "The Tale of the Captive Princess." His mother's project, for sure. He was glad he had decided not to leave it scattered. Page 14, page 5, page 11, page 2, page 12: The word *warriors* caught his eye.

The warriors poured forth from their boats, he read, *and made haste to the stronghold where the Fair One waited, pretending—*

"Hey! Jeremy!" Austin's voice, shrill and very near, made him drop the pages all over again. "What you doing in here, Jeremy?"

"M.Y.O.B!" Jeremy said through clenched teeth.

"What's that mean?" Austin pulled out a sheet of paper that had fluttered under the edge of the bed and handed it to his brother. "What you doing?" he asked again.

"Mind your own business," Jeremy said. He glanced down at the page: *And the queen of that land was hard of heart, and sent her to wash the linen—*

"Jeremy," Austin whined, "I want to play with your soldiers."

"No. You aren't supposed to. Mom said so."

"Pleeeease!"

"Go away, Austin." He saw his little brother's fingers tugging at a lock of hair. "Isn't it your bedtime?"

"I want to play with 'em again," Austin insisted. Suddenly, before Jeremy could stop him, Austin lunged for the papers, grabbed a handful, and ran with them to the other side of the room.

"Okay, okay!" Jeremy didn't want to be around when his mother found her manuscript all scrunched up. "Give those back and you can go into my room and get out one boxful, but that's all."

Austin tossed the pages in the middle of the bed and ran. Jeremy started over, putting them all in order, smoothing out the rumpled corners. Maybe he would like this story after all, the way his mother thought. He couldn't help reading a little here and there. The words took him away to a world like the one that he and Quinn imagined for their ancient warriors. It was neat, in a way, but it made him shiver. He half expected to see something about a ravine and a dark forest growing up the side of a mountain, or something creepy like that. Blinking, he tried to ignore all the descriptions and searched instead for the part he had been reading when Austin interrupted. He wondered if the two kings fighting to the death came before that part or after it. There it was: *The warriors poured forth from their boats and made haste to the stronghold where the Fair One waited, pretending to ready herself for—*

"Jeremy? How's the homework coming?" His father was on his way up the stairs. In a rush, he replaced his mother's project, grabbed his backpack, and made a dash for his own room. It wasn't going to be easy to concentrate on fractions.

⁘ *Ulf*

The air fairly sparkled in that morning after rain, and the sun softened the chill of it. A glory of autumn color stretched all up and down the river. The girl sang a little as she worked, but Ulf scarcely noticed, so intent was he on keeping his tongue in check. He knew without being told that he should say nothing of his conversation with the wizard. Yet he longed to tell it all to Gudrun, to hear comfort in her voice, to hear her reassurance that Harket must be mistaken about the dog. The effort of silence made his expression grim as he helped her wring another length of wet linen and stretch it over the bushes to dry.

"Ill temper will not change our fate, young Ulf," she chided him finally. Then he was ashamed to have shown her such a sour face, and the forbidden words of explanation rose up to his lips.

"I am glad to have this work," he began, "to keep me at your side. It is only that last night, the wizard—" In that instant, he saw a boat on the water, a sight so unexpected that the shock of it silenced him.

Beside him, Gudrun saw it, too, and stiffened. "Travelers," she murmured.

Ulf watched the slow approach of the little craft as it came upstream, watched as the two figures rowing took on the clear shape of young men. They scanned the bank warily. If they carried weapons, he could not see them, but even so, he worried that he would be of no help to the princess. What chance would an unarmed boy have against two such as these?

"Ho! Washerwoman!" shouted one of the travelers as the boat turned toward the riverbank. Ulf heard Gudrun draw breath sharply and stifle a cry. No wonder, he thought. It was punishment enough to have the noblewomen come to jeer at her, but it was worse still for strangers to think she was a common servant. She drew her shawl up over her hair and across her face.

"Stay!" the young man called as the boat came closer to shore. "Do not be afraid." Ulf could see now that they were outlanders, and both of high birth, for there was gold in the fastenings of their cloaks.

The one who spoke was tall and fair. "Whose lands are these?" he said.

Ulf opened his mouth to answer, but the girl touched his arm to stop him, and he felt the urgency in her fingers.

"Ludwig is the king who rules here," she said. Her voice came trembling through the shawl. "Ludwig and his son, Armut."

Ulf saw how the eyes of one traveler sought the eyes of the other, saw the look that flashed between them. He moved closer to Gudrun as the boat nosed against the bank. Both men alighted to secure it, and now they stood just paces away, at the edge of the huge, flat washing stone, searching the stream and the path with their eyes.

The second man, the one who had been silent, made a small noise in his throat. "Can you—" he began, and halted. He peered at the girl and began again. "Would you know if, some time ago, a king's daughter was brought here—against her will—from a northern land?" Ulf stared at him, at his strong square shoulders and his hair the color of sand.

"She was very fair of face," the traveler went on, "and very young. She would be young still."

"Do you know of her, washerwoman?" the tall one said. "Do you know if she lives or dies?"

Ulf heard the girl catch her breath and saw her pull the shawl away from her face.

"Orton!" Gudrun cried, reaching out her arms. "See? I live! Dear brother, I thought I knew your voice! And I knew you would come for me! I knew, always!"

Ulf had to scuttle backward as the other man, the square-shouldered one, rushed to stand before the girl and take her hands. "Gudrun!" he said, very low. "I never thought to see you again alive."

"Greetings to you, Erik of Zirn," she whispered, and color rose in her face.

Ulf gulped for air like a great fish above water. This was Erik, the one she was to wed. Erik of Zirn! Ulf turned his eyes to Orton, the royal brother, expecting that now he, too, would rush to Gudrun with arms outstretched. But he did not.

Orton did not move, and his cheeks grew red above his pale beard. "I would not believe it is you," he said finally to Gudrun, "had you not spoken my name." His eyes swept up and down her figure, from her tattered shawl to the disarray of her hair and back to the rough washerwoman's skirt muddied at the hem. "Your husband misuses you," he said, and there was cold fury in his voice.

Ulf saw how Gudrun held fast to the hand of her prince although she turned to face her brother. "I have no husband," she said. "Armut has not yet forced me to be wed to him. I have refused time and again, and so his mother treats me with loathing." She pointed to the linen hung about on the bushes. "All this is a punishment from Queen Erlinda, and it is only one of many. She makes me her servant."

"No more! Come away!" Erik urged. "The ships and warriors of our two lands lie just downstream." He tugged at her, stepping backward toward the place where the boat waited, bobbing gently with the current. "And you come, too, boy," he said to Ulf. "There is no need for you to stay here to tell our tale."

Ulf nodded and his heart thumped. It would be so simple, for him and for Gudrun, too. He could not have dreamed of so easy an escape. But before Ulf could draw a breath to speak his thanks, Gudrun's brother stepped back, blocking the way to the boat.

"Wait!" Orton said. "Listen to me!" And now he moved to touch the girl's cheek, and his eyes were bright with feeling. "Little sister," he said gently, "it would bring dishonor to our name if I took you away by stealth. Among our people, what is taken by force must be regained by force, and you know it well." He put up his hand to stay the sputtered protests of his companion.

"Hear me, Erik," he said. "My father's death must be avenged. If I do not take blood for it now, and if we do not reclaim my sister in the expected way, all these old wolves who rule along this river will think me faint of heart. They will come again and again to circle my keep. And your courage, too, will be questioned in many a warrior's camp if you make no show of taking back your betrothed."

Ulf scarcely breathed. He saw Gudrun's face give up the glow that had come to it.

Erik of Zirn scowled. "It is the safety of my betrothed that is in my mind," he said, beckoning Orton to go stand with him a little way off along the river. Ulf watched them there, and he could hear the growl of their argument but not the words. At last they fell silent, glaring at each other, and Gudrun sighed.

"So it is to be," she whispered. Ulf saw that her eyes were wet. "Would that I could fly away now," she said, "and be done with this place. But I have always known that blood must be shed."

Ulf nodded, remembering how she had told him and how he had not wanted to believe it. The girl straightened her shoulders as her brother approached, with Erik glowering behind him. Orton took his sister's hand, and Ulf marveled that his touch was so gentle when his eyes were so fierce.

"When I see our homeland again, dear sister, I will be made king in our father's stead. I promise you I will need every bit of honor to be gained in this encounter if I am to keep his power. Tomorrow we will come with all our warriors. Erik and I have agreed."

The prince of Zirn opened his mouth and then shut it, bowing his head stiffly to the brother of his betrothed.

Ulf could see no feeling at all on Gudrun's face. She raised one slender hand. "Ludwig's keep is yon way," she said, "up the stream and over the bank toward the sunrise. The watchmen guards are there, but no one else save the women and the children and the servants."

Orton scowled. "My quarrel is with Ludwig and his men."

"And the prince," muttered Erik.

Gudrun looked down at her feet. "The king is camped not far away, they say," she told them. "The men are hunting to bring meat for the winter."

"Ludwig must bring them home to us instead," said Orton. "Tomorrow!" And he leaned close to Gudrun's ear and whispered for a long time against her hair. Ulf saw the girl shiver, saw the color drain out of her face. At last, she nodded.

"Be strong, little sister," Orton said. "Do not leave the shelter of the keep on the morrow until I come for you." Again, she nodded.

Ulf's mouth was dry. He wondered how Gudrun would avoid the morning guard that brought them to the river. He thought of Orton's warriors and the men of Zirn who would snake their way through the ravine and up the hill to the keep. Something he could not name coiled itself in his stomach.

Orton pulled his sister closer, then, and kissed her forehead. "Do not fear," he said, and turned toward the river.

Erik of Zirn came to murmur something against her

cheek, and it left the shadow of a smile on both their faces as he took his leave.

"Should we take this lad with us then, to keep him quiet?" Erik said to Orton, and Ulf stepped backward, out of reach.

"Please, no," Gudrun said quickly. "Leave him with me, for courage. There would be questions if he is gone. He has a good heart and a good head—he will give no warning."

Ulf felt his face grow hot. She had praised him. He stared at the ground while the two men climbed into their boat and pushed it away from shore. For a long time, across the water, he could hear them arguing still, their voices low and intense.

"Ulf!" He looked up when the girl called his name. "Help me gather these," she said. She was pulling underskirts and kerchiefs from where they were spread, yanking them with no care for snags.

"But—but they are wet still," he protested, although he ran to help her.

"That is no matter!" Her laugh rang out high and clear. "No matter at all!" She dragged the wet garments across the washing stone to the edge of the river and flung them into the slow current one by one.

Ulf stood by with his mouth agape, unable to say a word. The queen would have her beaten, it was sure.

"Look, Ulf!" She opened out her arms to the river. "I am

a washerwoman no longer. Queen Erlinda's gowns are as free today as I shall be tomorrow!"

"The—the guard," Ulf stammered. "What will he say?"

"We will not wait for the guard," the girl said. When she turned to look at Ulf, all her laughter was gone, and her face was set. "I have much to do this day," she said, "and many lies to tell, and some of them will please the queen so much that she will forget to ask about her linen."

Gudrun strode away from the river and along the stream more like a warrior than a princess. Ulf followed behind, full of questions but without enough breath to ask even one. His mind raced with the speed of his feet as they hurried up the path through the edge of the forest, toward the keep. They would both have a beating this day, he thought, for coming in when the sun was still high, and empty handed. Maybe the queen would send for the rods and lay on the blows herself. And tomorrow—

"I do not see how the king and Prince Ar can do battle tomorrow when they are yet away," he said at last.

"They will be there," she said over her shoulder. "Before morning they all will be home."

"Are you like Old Berta?" he asked, puffing with the effort of their speed. "Are you able to know what you cannot see?"

The girl halted then as the path opened out to the brown meadow and the great house beyond. "No, Ulf," she said, whispering now, and her own breath was labored and her face was solemn. "There is no wizardry in me. I know only that I am the one who can make this thing happen, and it must happen today." Her eyes were on the keep. "So it is to be."

"Oh," said Ulf, but he could not see what she meant. He only saw how pale she was behind the flush on her cheeks. "I want to help you," he said. "I will ask the queen to give me all your blows as well as my own."

"Dear Ulf!" she said, and she put her hand for a moment on his shoulder. "Come with me and watch what happens, if you like, but I do not think you will see the rod. Stay to the shadows, and go to the wizard as soon as you can. You must warn him of the day to come." She bent her head then and put a sister's kiss on his bright hair.

Speechless and sad, he followed her through the silent grass and all the way to the din of the great hall, into the presence of the queen herself. And he saw that the girl was right. There was no beating. Ulf could have gone anywhere that day, done anything, stood on his head in the king's bedchamber, all without punishment. He might as well have been invisible. Every eye was on Gudrun the Fair, the outlander princess dressed like a washerwoman, pleading before the queen that she had felt a change of heart, begging that she be allowed to marry Prince Armut, and on the very next day, if only he could be called back so soon.

Ulf's head swam at the flurry of activity that followed. Gudrun disappeared into the arms of Princess Orrun and was led away amid a twittering of young noblewomen. Watchmen ran to the stables and galloped off to take the news, he supposed, to Ar and his father and the war troop. Frenzy broke out in the kitchen at the prospect of the troop's return and a wedding feast, all at once.

Ulf slipped out before the cook caught sight of him and made his way just at dark, lonely and heavy hearted, to the wizard's hut. He wondered if Harket had any power over the night, to make it stay. He did not know what the morrow would bring, but he did not think that, for him, it could bring any good.

Jeremy

Jeremy had forgotten that his parents were spending all day Saturday out of town.

"It's the big game, sport," his father said on Friday at breakfast. "You know we always go back to the campus and meet my old roommates and make a day of it."

"I guess so." Jeremy remembered that last year he had spent an entire day helping Mrs. Ramey entertain Austin in her big old dark museum of a house. He scowled at his little brother, who was slurping the milk off his cereal and handing the soggy little squares down to the dog, one by one. "Do I have to go back to Mrs. Ramey's with Austin?"

His mother shook her head. "Richelle's coming," she said, and then, "I must be out of my mind to have agreed to this trip this year. Five A.M.! Hour after hour on the free-way! And I could have my project in the mail by noon tomorrow if I could just stay home."

"No chance," her husband said cheerfully, not even looking up from his newspaper. "You need a break. And you always have fun once we get going."

"Please not Richelle," Jeremy said as soon as he could get in a word. "I don't care if she baby-sits Austin, but please, please don't put her in charge of me! Not without Quinn anyway."

"Watch it, Jeremy," his father said, changing his tone.

His mother just sighed. "Final instructions after school. Maybe things will be better than you think."

That little bit of hope got him through the day, even the test on fractions and the limp fish sticks in the cafeteria and the scrimmage at recess, when he was thinking about the boy in the ravine and it made him miss two easy passes in a row. But his mother was waiting in the parking lot when the bell rang, and she had good news.

"Quinn went back to school today," she said as Jeremy belted himself into the front seat and reached backward to give Austin a little poke for hello.

"No way!" he said. "Just last night Richelle said it might be days and days!" He didn't know whether to be excited or disgusted.

"That Richelle!" There was a smile in his mother's voice.

"She's a fussbudget sometimes. But that's what makes her such a good baby-sitter."

"Not for me," Jeremy said. "I'm too old for a baby-sitter."

"Me, too!" Austin pounded his own chest with both fists. "I'm a big guy!"

"Well," his mother said, "Richelle will come to our house and watch you, Austin, big guy or not. As a matter of fact, since we're leaving so early, and since the cable company is coming who knows when to install our new line, I've asked Richelle to come and spend the night."

"Unnh!" Jeremy didn't even try to muffle his groan.

"And you'll go spend the night with Quinn."

"All *right*!" Relief washed over him. At last they would get a chance to talk and plan.

"Quinn's dad will keep an eye on you, he says, and he'll be around if Richelle needs anything."

Thinking about Mr. DaSilva made Jeremy squirm just a little. What if he lectured them about the ravine? Or had a new, stricter set of rules for them to follow? But it couldn't be too bad, he reasoned, since he would be with Quinn. Finally!

Dinner that evening seemed to take forever, but then at last his father drove him to the DaSilvas' house and dropped him off with a pat on the shoulder and a warning to behave himself. Jeremy nodded. He didn't think a nod was quite as strong as a promise. His father was whistling his college fight song, so Jeremy knew he had his mind on other things anyway.

"Hey, Jeremy, what's up?" Quinn said as he opened the door.

"Just wait till you hear," said Jeremy under his breath. He saw Mr. DaSilva wave a greeting from the other side of the room without taking his eyes off his computer screen. Perfect! Jeremy thought. With Quinn's dad preoccupied, it would be just the two of them. "Listen!" he whispered. "Have I ever got stuff to tell you!"

"Like what?" Quinn reached for one of the boxes of warriors Jeremy had brought along to keep his mother from asking questions.

Jeremy didn't want to say anything that Quinn's dad might hear. "Come on," he said, starting toward the basement. "We'd better get the battle set up if we're going to play." Together they clattered down toward their familiar hangout.

"You're okay now, aren't you?" Jeremy asked on the stairs, and then he said, "I'm glad," without even waiting for an answer. "Listen, Quinn," he said, "I've figured it out. We can go down in the ravine anytime we want—if we really have to, I mean—just as long as Duchess isn't there. I tried it, like an experiment, see? First I went down the hill by myself and it was okay, but then I took her with me and I ended up somewhere else, just like before. And I saw this short kid and he tried to call Duchess but he didn't know her name, and then he ran at us and hollered, and I got out of there fast!"

"Huh?" Quinn said. He settled himself on the shag carpet alongside the battle board with an expression that made Jeremy feel as if he had just turned into an alien.

"What do you mean, 'Huh'?" Jeremy shook his head. "*You* know. I'm talking about what happened last Saturday in the ravine. I tried it again."

Quinn shook his head. "Well, I kept dreaming stuff about the ravine," he said. "Like I thought we saw one of our warriors on a horse down there. My dad laughed when I told him."

"You *told* him?"

"He said my fever was so high I was delirious already, but we'd better stay out of the ravine or we'd both be grounded, because there's some old guy who—"

"Yeah, I know," said Jeremy, interrupting. "Richelle already told me." He stared at Quinn's bent head, and he felt betrayed. "Listen, *I* wasn't delirious! It *happened*, Quinn. Believe me." He dropped to his knees on the other side of the battle board and opened the box of skirmishers he was still carrying. He needed to keep his hands busy. "You didn't tell your dad about the knife, too, did you?"

"Oh, yeah. Right." Quinn laughed and lowered his voice. "Uh, gee, Dad, I forgot to mention that Great-grandpa's dagger with the gold inlay on the handle just happens to be in a hole in the ground down in the ravine."

Jeremy smiled in spite of himself. "We have to get it back," he said. "And I know we can do it. As long as Duchess isn't with us, nothing strange will happen."

"Aw, Jeremy, relax!" Quinn got up and brought a can of soda for each of them from the little refrigerator in the corner. "Forget about that weird stuff we thought we saw, and let's get our battle lines set up."

"What do you mean, we *thought* we saw?"

"Didn't you ever hear of hallucinations? Or optical illusions? Or—or delirium? Or getting so wrapped up in a game that it starts to seem real?" Quinn's hands moved fast, setting out archers in front of his heavy weaponry. "Be logical, Jeremy!"

"Yes, but—" Jeremy had heard every word clearly, but still he couldn't understand. How could Quinn act as if everything were still normal? Maybe the fever had really affected his mind. If he could just have seen what happened the other day in the rain . . .

"Come on!" Quinn poked at the box in front of Jeremy. "Hurry up with your skirmishers."

"Okay, okay." Jeremy tried to think while his unsteady hands sent ancient warriors falling askew across the battle board. Maybe it didn't matter what Quinn believed or didn't believe, just as long as they recovered the knife safely. He managed to get his men in order and take his turn rolling the dice.

"So here's what we could do," Jeremy said as casually as his tight chest would allow. "Tomorrow we watch for our chance. And then when no one is watching, we go dig up the knife and bring it back here and you could put it back in the chest, and we wouldn't have to say anything to anyone."

"Okay," agreed Quinn. "We have to do it, but it shouldn't be hard. It'll be easy. Just like this!" And he laughed at the lucky roll that let his archers cut down half a rank of Jeremy's men.

"Rats!" said Jeremy, and he felt a little of his anxiety slipping away into the game. Here he was, with Quinn again, and without Richelle to bother them. There were plenty of snacks, and he was sleeping over. Why shouldn't he feel good? Tomorrow, finally, they would settle the business of the knife, and then the ravine wouldn't have to matter anymore. But however much he talked to himself, he couldn't get over his disappointment. He had counted on Quinn to reassure him, to help him figure things out, but it wasn't happening. Quinn was no help at all.

By Mr. DaSilva's orders, they spent that night in Quinn's room on real beds and turned off the TV before midnight. They slept all the way to daylight, and then crept downstairs to get cereal, taking care not to wake Quinn's father. If he got up too early, he would be in no mood to cook the big breakfast they were hoping for later.

But in the kitchen, there were no signs of a big breakfast to come. There was a note, instead, printed out on neon-yellow paper. "Boys," they read, heads together over the counter. "Sorry but you will have to find your own food. Plenty in refrig. I will be at station all day—have to fill in for someone. Don't forget to check in with Richelle. Call me if it's an emergency."

Jeremy looked at the telephone number below the words and began to grin. "We're free!" he crowed.

Quinn stretched and reached for the cereal. "Yeah, and we've got all day."

"But let's not wait," Jeremy said, taking the milk out of the refrigerator. "Let's go get the knife right now and put it back and make sure everything's okay, and then we really will have all the rest of the day with nothing left to worry about." He was certain that nothing odd would happen in the ravine unless Duchess was there, but even so, the thought of climbing down the embankment all the way to the fort made him feel shaky. He wanted to get it over with. It would be some comfort, he thought, if only Quinn realized how dangerous it could be. But no amount of talk last night had been able to convince Quinn that what he remembered about the horse in the ravine was more than a dream.

"Let's not wait," Jeremy said again. "Okay? Please? Let's get it over with."

"Okay, already!" Quinn yawned and made a face. "Anything to keep you from yapping the rest of the day." He smiled and handed Jeremy a spoon.

They both gulped their cereal, racing each other to the bottom of the bowl, and then they pulled on their zippered sweatshirts and went out into the morning. Jeremy put his hands in the pockets for warmth and pulled them out again. He had forgotten that he had hidden some of his warriors there—all the royal troop commanders, the heavy pewter ones as well as the plastic—to keep them away from Austin.

"Come on," urged Quinn. "You were in such a hurry. Let's run. Last one to the fort has to do the digging."

Jeremy kept up with Quinn better than either of them could have predicted. Probably, Jeremy thought, it was because Quinn had been sick, or maybe it was because he, Jeremy, was so nervous that he felt supercharged. The sky was overcast and the neighborhood was quiet except for the sound of their shoes pounding along toward the end of Quinn's street. They both had to slow a little as they continued through the high grass along the edge of the ravine, looking for the spot halfway down where the clump of bushes grew around the fort. When Jeremy spotted it, he could also see the gold and purple and red of the late chrysanthemums in Mrs. Ramey's garden. It should have been comforting to be so close to home.

"I'm winning!" Quinn shouted, disappearing over the edge of the ravine. Jeremy had to stop and remind himself that everything was all right before his legs would take him down the hill to catch up.

"Watch out for that guy and his horse," Quinn warned, laughing. He held back the bushes to let in enough light for Jeremy to find the stones where the knife was buried.

"Don't joke," Jeremy said, trying not to tremble. "It isn't funny." He began to dig, using the sharp end of a broken branch.

"Lighten *up*," Quinn said. "You don't see anything weird here today, do you?"

Jeremy stopped scrabbling in the dirt long enough to take a look around. He had to admit that everything seemed normal. Still, he wanted to finish and get out of the ravine as soon as possible. So he dug faster, using his hands and the edge of one of the flat stones, ignoring all of Quinn's comments about hearing hoofbeats.

There! There was the earth-stained T-shirt that protected the belt and the scabbard, with the dagger inside. He unfolded the cloth and pulled the knife out, slowly, smiling in relief. It seemed to be in perfect condition. No blemishes, no rust. The blade still shone.

"All *right*!" Quinn said, serious at last. "Come on. I'll

carry it. Leave the shirt down here, though. Look at all those slimy little bug-things on the sleeve."

Jeremy shrugged, but he dropped the fake chain mail fast and brushed his hands off on the seat of his jeans. He was sorry that such a great shirt was too dirty to save.

"Hey, Quinn," he said. "You shouldn't carry that knife out in plain sight. We didn't see anyone coming down here, but we might on the way back. Like Mrs. Ramey— she'd have a royal fit."

Quinn frowned. "Yeah, I know. But it's too big for any of my pockets."

"Fasten the belt way up under your arms and wear the scabbard here." Jeremy patted his own chest. "*Under* your jacket. It's only for a little way." He thought of the gleam of the blade, and for a moment he wished that he could be the one with the dagger strapped against his body.

"Good idea," Quinn said. "I'll belt it up under my sweatshirt." He fussed with the buckle. "There isn't anyone around, is there?"

"Nobody, Quinn. I swear." Jeremy made an effort to keep his voice calm. "All we have to do now is go up the bank and straight to your house. Okay?"

"Come on," Quinn said. "Race you to the top.

They crashed back upward through weeds and over fallen branches, not pausing until they stood on the edge, looking back into the ravine. Jeremy's breath came in little short puffs, but he felt wonderful.

Quinn was beaming. "I told you it wasn't going to be any big deal!" He raised his hand, palm outward, to meet Jeremy's in a high five of celebration.

In the very instant that Jeremy felt Quinn's hand slap against his own, his eye caught a blur of movement at the near side of Mrs. Ramey's garden. A streak of white and golden tan wove through the bright chrysanthemums, straight for the ravine's edge. The back of Jeremy's neck felt cold and hot and cold again. Surely it couldn't be Duchess. *No way.* Then he saw a little figure pumping along in pursuit, with copper hair plain as a name tag. Before Jeremy could take a breath, his dog had disappeared down the embankment and his little brother after her.

"Austin! AUSTIN!" Jeremy had barely thought about the possibility that someone else might go into the ravine with Duchess. He had never imagined his little brother would be the one in danger. *"Austin, come back!"* he shrieked.

Quinn put his hands over his ears. "What the—"

Jeremy spun his friend around just in time for both of them to see Richelle, running faster than they thought Richelle could run.

"Austin!" she called. "Austin, come up here! I'll get her! It's not your fault, Austin! The cable guy left the gate open!" She slowed down at the ravine's edge, but she didn't stop.

For just a moment, Jeremy felt as if he had turned to

stone. His heart didn't beat, his lungs were still. Panic came up into his throat, and then suddenly his breath came.

"Wait!" he yelled. "Richelle, come back! You don't *know*!" He ran, pulling at Quinn's arm, and Quinn followed. In a moment they were over the edge, following Duchess and Austin and Richelle down the embankment, deep into the ravine. It was dark there, dark as midnight, and the air was cold, and somewhere far off a wolf was howling.

✦ *Ulf*

Sleep would not come to Ulf that night, even after the wizard and his wife were finished with their singing and no more threads of smoke came from behind their curtain. He lay this way and that, but his eyes would not close. At last he got up and crept outside to sit on the wizard's stump along the doorpath, taking comfort from the familiar stars overhead. He wished the day ahead could be as easy to foretell as the slow, sure coming of the moon.

He had told the wizard every detail of what he had heard—of Gudrun's brother, Prince Orton, and of Prince Erik of Zirn, and how their warriors would march to the keep, while Gudrun the Fair had called for Prince Ar to come home, saying she would marry him. Old Berta had frowned at that. "Surely not of her own will," she muttered.

"There will be battle, regardless," the wizard had said. "You can count on it, boy. If you are near to it, you will be swept into the arms of your mother. None can protect you from Gudrun's people but the princess herself, and none who serve Erlinda will give your head a second thought. Do not go near the keep tomorrow."

Berta had agreed. "If any come for you, I will turn them away," she promised. Ulf protested, shaking his head until he was dizzy, but nothing would change the wizard's mind.

Just past dark, they had heard Ludwig's war troop clattering through the ravine, riling Berta's geese with their whooping and shouting, already celebrating the wedding-to-be of Prince Ar. Now, under the night sky and with the lonely song of a faraway wolf in his ears, Ulf tried to think of all that might happen and what he should do.

He wondered where Gudrun the Fair would lay her head when the next night fell, whether it would be on a ship bound for Zirn or on a marriage bed in the household where she had already known so much unhappiness. Worst of all, he thought, she might perish in the battle her brother insisted he must fight to save her. Would he see Gudrun ever again? Ulf's head ached with the effort of such thoughts, and his ears began to play tricks, bringing him strange voices through the night.

"Oh, I'm so glad you boys are here! I've never been so frightened in my life. What is it anyway? An eclipse?"

"Man, Jeremy, what's the deal here? This is really creepy. I don't like it. Let's go back."

"No, Quinn! I told you last night! We can't get back without Duchess. So the first thing we have to do is find her. And we have to get Austin. He's just a little kid, and he's lost!"

"But so are we, Jeremy!"

"Ow! Ooh! I've twisted my ankle. Ow! I can't walk!"

"Help her, Jeremy! Take her other arm!"

"No, you stay here with her while I go find Austin. We can't let him and the dog get too much of a head start."

"You're never going to find them in the dark! You don't even know which way they went."

"Don't you dare go off by yourself, Jeremy! Not after I've already lost your little brother. Oh, where are we anyway?"

For a while, Ulf thought the night air had lulled him, that he might have fallen into a dream. The voices were young and the sounds were nonsense; they brought no threat to him. But none of the children he knew dared to come near the wizard's hut in daylight—certainly not in the dark of night. After a little time, he began to hear beyond the alien language to the meaning beneath, and he remembered with wonder the ill-tasting charm Berta had given him. He got up from the stump where he sat and went toward the sounds, for he could recognize distress, whatever the accent.

He saw them before they saw him, and it gave him time

to swallow some of his astonishment. There were three of them standing very close together on the bank of the stream. The tallest one had the form of a girl, although she seemed to have long coverings on her legs just like the others. He had seen travelers now and again as visitors in the queen's household, but none, ever, in garments of such outlandish shape. The girl stood on one leg, leaning against one of the boys.

"This really hurts," she said.

Ulf made the sign against evil, just in case, and took two loud steps toward them. "Do you need someone to help you?" he asked. He thought of the warriors who, at some dark hour, would follow Prince Orton and Erik of Zirn up the ravine to rescue Gudrun from the keep. "There may be danger along this stream tonight," he said.

The three figures went stiff as trees on a windless day. Finally one of the boys nudged the other one forward. "You do the talking, Jeremy," he said very low.

"Jere-my?" repeated Ulf, and the sound of it was awkward on his tongue. "I am Ulf."

"G-g-glad to—to meet you," the boy in front said, with a voice that wavered like an owl's. "And, uh, this is Quinn, and—and his sister, Richelle. And I'm—Jeremy. Hi." He raised one hand and waved it just a little, a motion that Ulf could barely see as a thin cloud dimmed the rising moon. Still, it was enough.

"I remember!" Ulf said. "I saw you on the hill." He caught his breath. "With the dog!" So these were the powerful, unfriendly creatures from Magic's world. He would have laughed if they had not seemed so lost and frightened.

"Come and talk to the wizard," he said. "Please. Please! It is just a little way up the path here."

"Wizard?" The girl moaned a little. "What wizard?"

"I'm sorry, but we can't," Jeremy said, stepping closer, and Ulf could hear his voice grow steadier word by word. "We can't go anywhere until you tell me if you saw my dog today. I mean, tonight. Just a few minutes ago. She got away from our yard, see, and my brother was chasing her to bring her back, and he's just a little guy—" With two fingers, Jeremy marked the place on his ribs where Austin's head reached when they stood side by side. "Have you seen him, maybe? He's lost now, in the dark"—Jeremy swallowed—"and we don't any of us know where we are."

"The dog has come here again?" Ulf could not hide his surprise. No wonder he had not been able to sleep, he thought.

"Maybe she's with Austin and she'll take care of him," the girl said, and then she hid her face in her hands.

"Your dog has come here before," Ulf said urgently to Jeremy. "The queen has heard of it and of her great beauty. The story is told that it is no dog, but a golden wolf."

"*What?*" Jeremy's mouth hung open.

"Your dog does not look like our dogs," Ulf said. "And the queen wants it for her own, to keep in a cage, she says, or to—" He stopped.

"To what?" Jeremy was shaking.

"To wear," Ulf said, very softly, so the girl would not hear, "to wear its fur around her neck."

"Duchess? *No!*" Jeremy began to pace back and forth across the entrance to Harket's doorpath. "Imagine what a person who could think of something like that might do to Austin," he said. "I've got to find them!"

In the moonlight, Ulf could see the panic on the other boy's face, and he reached for him, to keep him from running. "No," he said. "Please. Come with me, all of you. We will wake the wizard. He will know what to do."

Ulf herded them all up the path as if they were Berta's geese, although the girl leaned on her brother and was very slow. But they did not have to wake the wizard. He was waiting for them, filling the doorway with his presence, from the flowing white of his hair to the dark sweep of the hem of his cloak.

"Come in, children," Harket said gently. "Come in."

❖ *Jeremy*

It was the smallest house that Jeremy had ever seen, just one tiny room lit by the flicker of a sputtering fire. He thought they were not all going to fit into it, but the man with the beard—the wizard, he supposed—insisted. An old woman came from behind a curtain in the corner to help Richelle get settled on a bench with her leg stretched out. After the old woman sat opposite her, the only place left for the boys was on the floor. Animal hides over hard-packed earth, Jeremy guessed. It was lumpy and uncomfortable.

Everything seemed so dark, so strange. Who wouldn't be afraid? Jeremy thought, trying to reason with himself. He swallowed against the fear that rose up in his throat. He couldn't be sick. Not here. Not now. He had to concentrate on finding Austin and the dog. That boy, Ulf, had said something about danger by the stream. Austin would be needing help, and fast. And Duchess, too, if someone really wanted to capture her. He swallowed again. This was no time to be afraid.

Beside him, Quinn kept twitching his nose. Jeremy understood. The room was smoky, heavy with unfamiliar scents, too warm and close for regular breathing. He un-zipped his jacket and tried to catch Quinn's eye, but Quinn stared straight ahead. His friend's face was as pale as on the night they had rented horror movies and watched four in a row. He wished Quinn would say something, or even just look at him—anything to balance out the way the other boy was studying the both of them. At least this Ulf seemed friendly enough. Hadn't Duchess wagged her tail at him just the other day? The memory made Jeremy shudder.

Just then the wizard leaned forward from his seat by the hearth. "I am Harket," he said, each word slow and deliberate, "and this is Berta, my wife. No harm will come to you within these walls." Jeremy thought he felt Quinn relax just a little beside him, but Richelle straightened her shoulders.

"You must return to your home," the old man said, looking at each one in turn. "You have parents, I think, who will be looking for you."

"In just a few hours, they will. Or—or anytime now." It was Richelle who spoke up, although her voice was quivering. "I was supposed to be in charge," she said, "so if you have to—to do something dreadful to someone, it should be me."

The wizard murmured reassurance, but Jeremy glanced at Richelle with new respect. He hadn't ever thought of her as brave before. Still, she couldn't keep her shoulders from shaking. The old woman moved like a shadow and offered the girl something in a stone cup. Jeremy thought Richelle would be smart enough to push it away, but she drank from it instead. It was going to put her to sleep, he just knew it. Right when they needed all the help they could get! He waited while his heart beat once and then twice. Maybe Quinn would take over now, he thought. By this time, his friend should have figured out what to say to the wizard, how to get them some help. But nothing came out of Quinn's mouth at all. It's me or nobody, Jeremy thought, and he took a big breath.

"Mr. Harket," he said, "my little brother is here somewhere, lost. We have to find him. And our dog is here, too, and we can't go back to where we live unless she's with us. I mean, it's like she brought us here, somehow, and she'll have to take us back." Jeremy heard the old woman suck in her breath, but he kept his eyes on the wizard's face, which was very still. "At least that's what I think, sir." He closed his mouth tight to keep his chin from trembling and watched a look pass between Harket and the boy.

Then the old man turned to the fire and spoke into it, and bent so low above it that Jeremy was afraid the long beard would burst into flame. Finally the wizard straightened. "You must go find them, boy," he whispered. "But beware of the warriors, the archers and swordsmen of Zirn and the best men of Gudrun's homeland. It is their time."

Jeremy swallowed. The name Gudrun echoed in his memory, but he couldn't think why. "What do you mean?" he said, and his voice squeaked. Was this the danger Ulf had mentioned? His mind began to picture archers and swordsmen, and his fingers went automatically to the familiar shapes in his pocket. Their tiny weapons were sharp to the touch.

"Ulf will be your companion." The wizard continued as

if he had not heard any question. "He knows where the battle will be and how to keep out of the way of it."

"Battle?" Jeremy asked. "Like real fighting, you mean?"

"Ulf can help you with the dog," Harket went on. "She has come to his call before."

When? thought Jeremy. Had that boy been trying to steal his dog, or what? But he knew better than to complain. He needed Ulf.

Jeremy stood up on unsteady legs and pulled at Quinn's jacket sleeve. "My friend is coming, too. Okay?" Asking for Richelle would be hopeless, he could see that. She was resting her head on the table alongside the bench, not quite sleeping, not quite awake. She couldn't help them much anyway, he realized, not as long as her ankle hurt. But he couldn't go without Quinn. For this, for archers and swordsmen, for a *battle*, he had to have a friend. It didn't matter that Quinn wasn't himself right now. They were still best buddies, weren't they?

The wizard was nodding at Jeremy. "Listen well," he said. "We want you to find the little boy. We want you to find the dog. We want you to go home safely. All of you." His voice fell so low that Jeremy had to bend toward him, had to breathe in the very air the wizard breathed. "You must never visit us again," the old man said. "There is danger here for you. And you will bring danger to us if your people find a way to follow you."

Jeremy blinked his eyes against the intensity of the wizard's gaze. "Honest, Mr. Harket, sir, we don't want to make any trouble." He was whispering, talking fast. "We just want to go home. We didn't really mean to come here anyway, not to bother you. It was sort of like . . . an accident. Or something. I don't know exactly."

The wizard nodded silently, and Jeremy thought that he might be smiling. When the old man reached forward, Jeremy trembled at the quick, light touch on his shoulder and the sudden tingling that swept clear down to his toes.

"Go," said Harket.

Jeremy nodded and backed away, pulling Quinn, and they stumbled out the door together, into moonlight and shadow. He rubbed his eyes. Oh, Austin, he thought, where are you? Duchess, where are you? Maybe this was just a really bad dream after all, and he would wake up now. Please. Maybe Quinn would get his act together and quit staring straight ahead like the number-one zombie of the universe. But Quinn just kept right on standing beside him, silent and unmoving. Please, thought Jeremy again. Nothing changed, except that the wizard's door opened once more and Ulf came out.

"We have to hurry," he said. "There is not much time."

CHAPTER 11

⋯ *Ulf*

Ulf led the search for the child he had never seen and for the other boy's dog, for Magic, who should have been his own heart's companion. The sadness of it made him slow as they picked their way through the ravine, and the chance of meeting Prince Orton's troops made him wary. It did not help that the tall boy, Quinn, had to be poked and prodded along. Jeremy pulled him by the arm while he called in a low voice for the lost ones. Between the calls and whistles, when Ulf knew the boy should have listened with all his senses, Jeremy asked question after question. Where was this place? Why was there going to be a battle? Who was going to fight in it? Ulf was not accustomed to so much talk from someone his age. The answers Jeremy wanted were clear enough in Ulf's mind, but he could not think where to start the explanations.

"Wait," he said at last. "Keep your questions. Let me tell it from the beginning." Ulf took the lead along the water, then, from rock to rock and over logs and through the bushes that were as familiar to him as the fingers of his hand. As they went, he told how Gudrun had been stolen from her homeland and her father killed. Like a teller in the great hall singing a story, he repeated how she had been brought to King Ludwig's land to marry Prince Ar, who was weary now with her refusals. His voice grew hard when he spoke of Queen Erlinda and her cruelty, but softened when he told of Princess Orrun and her friendship for the captured girl.

Ulf's words, which so often were halting and slow, came rushing out of him now, and he was proud, for Jeremy made sounds of astonishment at several points in his telling. "King Ludwig!" he said once, plain and clear. "Quinn, it's King *Ludwig*! Remember?"

Ulf smiled and would not let himself be interrupted. He had found a little enjoyment in this bad night, and he wanted to keep it as long as he could—this willing audience of other boys. For once, he had companions. Just for now, he was not lonely. But then he came to the part of the story that told of Prince Orton and Erik of Zirn planning to bring their warriors through the ravine to the keep.

"Their men have been waiting in boats on the river for all of a day," Ulf said, "and maybe more. And this morning, when the light breaks, maybe even before, they will be coming out of their boats and up the stream and—"

"Wait a minute!" Jeremy broke in. "What did you say?"

Ulf stopped and looked back at him because the voice he used was so urgent.

"I—I thought I heard that somewhere before," Jeremy said.

Ulf frowned. How could that be? "And they will march to the keep," he went on, "where Gudrun the Fair pretends to wait for her marriage to Prince Ar, but in truth she waits for rescue, and—"

"The Fair One!" Jeremy cried. "Gudrun is the Fair One! Is she—"

Ulf interrupted the question that Jeremy began, for telling the story had reminded him how near they were to danger at this moment.

"Come this way," Ulf said abruptly, leading toward the steep path that went up through the forest's edge to the queen's orchard. The climbing left no breath for talk, so that the little boy's name, when Jeremy called it, was hardly more than a whisper. Jeremy's friend added his low whistle now from time to time. Ulf hoped the sound would bring nothing more than a dog. This was the wood gatherers' path, after all, but even so he thought it the safest. Better to meet Puli in the first light of morning than to be caught among the warriors who might even now be making their way toward the keep by the wider path nearer the river.

Ulf came to the top of the embankment and began to guide the others through the fir branches that hid the path there both night and day. Suddenly he was motionless, listening. From somewhere far away—ahead of them, he thought—came a faint flurry of noise. He wanted it to be the sound of a dog barking, but he couldn't be certain. He thought there was a distant shout and other cries of higher pitch, but all of it faded too soon and fell away.

"What's wrong?" Jeremy said, moving closer to him, but Ulf held up his hand for silence. And into that silence, down in the ravine behind them, came a different set of sounds—the chink of metal, the soft clatter of hooves, muffled voices.

Quinn stood so close to Jeremy that in the dark they seemed to be one boy with two heads, one above the other. "What *is* that?" Quinn said.

"Ancient warriors," Jeremy breathed in a voice so low that Ulf could hardly hear it. "An army on the march, Quinn."

An army far bigger than Ludwig's war troop, Ulf thought. An army big enough to claim a princess, he hoped. He felt a chill at the back of his neck, a prickling of excitement and dread.

Jeremy touched his arm. "Come on! Please! We have to

find Austin—you know, my little brother. What if he gets in their way or something? He won't have a chance!"

Ulf nodded. He knew well enough what danger there was for a little boy found in the way of oncoming raiders. "We will take this path through the trees," he said, "and maybe we will come to him."

In truth, Ulf's mind rested more on the dog than on the boy. He thought this path might take them to the dog, although he did not mention the sound that might have been barking. He hoped no harm had befallen the animal already. When he thought of Magic, of her clear gray eyes and her tall plume of a tail, a great heaviness came over him. It was not just that he was never to have her for his own, but that she herself was in such danger, such an easy target. Everyone who served the queen's household wanted to be the one who would bring the golden wolf to Erlinda. He listened again for the dog, but all he could hear now was the heavy progress of the army through the ravine below.

"Keep calling, but soft," he said to the others as they moved away from the bank of the ravine. "This path takes us toward the queen's orchard, but it should keep us away from the soldiers, I think." The dog had come to him once on this path. Her nose would surely remember it. But he did not speak this thought aloud.

For what seemed a long time, Ulf and his companions

made their way from one ragged patch of moonlight to another, searching among the trees and thickets, finding nothing but an owl and some little night creatures that skittered quickly away. Ulf felt the air grow colder as the darkness thinned to gray. He could hear Jeremy and Quinn shivering. He knew they were too cold to talk and too tired to walk any faster. He felt the same way.

"The queen's orchard is just ahead," he said, to encourage them. "When we come to the edge of these trees, we'll be able to see the meadow, all the way from the keep to the far mountain. If the little boy is there, or the dog, it will be easier to find them."

But even Ulf was not prepared for the sight that spread before them as the path led out of the forest's edge. He stepped into the open, drew one huge breath, and stepped back again into the shelter of the trees. His companions hurried to peer over his shoulders, one on each side. He was glad for them to be there, glad not to be alone. Beyond the bare orchard, in a great ragged circle as far around the walls of the keep as could be seen, the warriors from the north pressed inward against the men of Ludwig's war troop. They wrestled and smote and hacked and sliced in a tumult more dreadful than Ulf had imagined. He heard Jeremy breathe out a sound of distress, and beside him, Quinn said words to himself that Ulf could not understand. The fighting raged forward and back; the circle gave way, formed again, pulled tighter. Shouts and groans, the shrilling of horses, and the ringing of swords came muffled on the morning air.

The boys watched and listened, barely breathing, not looking at one another. Finally, Ulf felt his stomach churning. The noise of battle went deep into him and called to mind the screaming and the flames of his mother's village. He had to turn away, back to the soft gloom of the path along which they had come.

And that was when his eyes caught a flash of white, a glimpse of fur on an animal's chest. He knew it was Magic. She was almost hidden, some way off among the trees. In a moment he could see a child beside her, a child with hair the color of glowing embers. And then he realized, almost too late, that a huge shape towered over both of the lost ones. It was the morning watchman, the ill-tempered one whose task it had been to take Gudrun to the river. Ulf's heart sank within him. The watchman held both child and dog close to him on tether straps that looped around their necks.

"Quick!" Ulf whispered, reaching back for the others, who still gaped at the spectacle beyond the orchard. "Hide! Behind the thicket there! Make sure he doesn't see you!" He had to yank at them to get their attention, and then, when Jeremy saw his brother, Ulf had to restrain him from rushing to the rescue. He knew this watchman well enough to know that Jeremy stood no chance against him. None of them did.

Crouched behind the thicket with one hand on each of his companions, Ulf could not think what to do. He had seen the muzzle strap on the dog—poor Magic, he thought—but even so he worried that she might sniff them out and give away their hiding place. Meanwhile, the watchman drew closer, coming onto the path and grunting at his captives to hurry. Ulf guessed the man had heard the sounds of battle and was rushing to see what had caused such a fray.

Jeremy's body was taut as a bowstring beside him. "Oh, no," he kept whispering. "No, no, oh, no."

"If I were stronger," Ulf said under his breath, "I would take this sharp stone pressing into my belly and throw it at that oaf!"

"I could do that," Quinn offered suddenly, a bit too loud, and Jeremy said, "Yeah, Quinn, you could! You're the best thrower ever." Immediately the dog acknowledged their voices with a strangled bark.

Ulf shuddered. Through the branches of the thicket he could see the watchman slow his steps and then stop, examining both sides of the path before moving on. Ulf breathed slowly as the heavy steps resumed. The little boy walked by almost close enough to touch, winding his fingers through his hair.

"Maybe if we are behind him . . ." Ulf whispered, for no other idea came to him. "Maybe if he doesn't see us . . ." He had no stomach for telling the others how easily the watchman would kill them. After all, the watchman thought he had found the golden wolf and another prize as well. He would not want to give up such things before he could take them to the queen. *If* he could take them to the queen, Ulf thought, for a great shout came echoing from the battle around the keep.

The watchman had reached the place where the path broke into the open, near the orchard, and he stopped all at once and began to curse. "What treachery is this?" he shouted.

Staying low behind the thicket, Ulf grasped the stone and crept closer, motioning the others to follow. Maybe now was the time, although he worried about the strap around the child's neck. He did not have a chance to think how to get it off, for someone came running through the orchard, calling "Da! Da!" at the top of his voice.

"Puli? Is that you, Puli?" the watchman bellowed.

Quinn reached for the stone in Ulf's hand, but Ulf fended him off. The big man held the child too close. And now there was Puli, too, a second enemy.

"What happens here, my son?" the watchman said to Puli.

"Look to the keep, Da! Just see what these outlanders

have done to take back their princess! I knew that wizard's boy was a spy for her, with all that ugly yellow hair!"

"The wizard's boy, you say?"

Ulf was flat to the ground now. He did not know which of them—father or son—would most enjoy putting an end to him.

"Is that you?" Jeremy whispered. "Are you the wizard's boy?" Ulf nodded without looking around. His eyes were fixed on the watchman, who looked down at the dog and at Jeremy's brother.

"Well, these two will bring some spirit back to the queen," the watchman said, shaking the thick straps under his son's nose.

"No!" Puli cried. "I was in the great hall, and I saw her put to the sword! The invaders have killed the king, and they have killed her, too! The queen is dead!"

Ulf felt suddenly weak. "The queen is dead!" he repeated to himself, to make it seem real. But the relief that flooded through him was soon followed by dismay. The watchman might be dumbfounded at this moment, yet soon he could go into a rage over his own loss, punishing those who had seemed such a treasure and now were useless to him.

Ulf gathered his courage and passed the stone to Quinn. They would have to take a chance on getting the straps out of the watchman's big hand. He refused to think of the hopelessness of it. "Take them and run for the wizard's hut while I—" He blocked the thought of Puli and his fists. Maybe he could be like an insect, he thought, stinging and darting away. "Now!" he said sharply to the others, scrambling to his feet.

The watchman turned at the sound of Ulf's voice, and he raised his club. But before he could strike, there were hoofbeats and shouts at the edge of the orchard, a blur of noise and motion.

Ulf checked his own forward rush. The other boys hesitated with him at the edge of the path, their eyes on the watchman, who seemed to lurch backward into the open and then plunge to the ground, with the shaft of an arrow rising out of his chest. Beside his father, Puli also shrieked and fell, and lay still. The child began to wail in a voice that Ulf could not bear to hear. The dog was nowhere to be seen. For a moment the little boy seemed to step free, and then he, too, disappeared entirely from Ulf's sight. Jeremy bolted away and started to crash through the underbrush.

"Wait!" cried Ulf, catching the other boy by the arm. His companions had no idea how foreign they looked, or what danger their appearance might bring upon their own heads. "Stay here," he said to both of them as it grew quieter on the path beyond the trees. "Watch, but do not be seen. What would we say if any questioned you? I will be the one to go and look." And Ulf walked as boldly as he could into the open, stepping over the fallen Puli and his father as if he were no stranger to such sights, as if he saw lifeblood spilled on the ground every day.

Two men were a little way off in the early morning sun, two men with the pale hair of northern lands and the easy air of victory. One of them was on foot, and he had the dog, holding her tether strap while he worked to remove the muzzle. Ulf knew that she sensed his own presence; her tail, matted as it was with burrs and twigs, began to swing side to side.

"Look at this dog," said the man to his companion, who was on horseback. "She favors me already."

The horseman laughed and swung his mount around. Ulf took a deep breath. There sat Jeremy's little brother between the rider's knees, free of his neck strap but tight in the man's grip. "You should give that dog to our new princess of Zirn," the horseman said. "It would make almost as fine a marriage gift as this little pup that I will give her. She can train this one up to serve her however she wants." He tousled the child's bright hair, and Ulf marveled at the strength of the boy's outcry. The rider scowled and gave the howling face a smack.

Ulf heard himself shout at the same moment he heard the dog growl. "Rider!" he cried, and ran to put himself between the dog and the target of her displeasure. "Why take one so little?" He knew how it felt, every bit of it—the blows, the fright, the loneliness. It was nothing but terror for one so small; sometimes he remembered, though never by choice.

"Why take that one, who will cause you so much trouble, when I would go willingly in his place?" The words came to Ulf before he knew he intended to say them, but as their meaning settled on him, eagerness gathered in his voice. "I would serve your princess, and gladly," he said. "And I am strong already, at least a bit." He flexed one scrawny arm. "And I am willing to learn new tasks, and I will not complain, and—" He was running out of breath. The little boy stared at him.

The horseman, who had looked him over with a fierce expression at the beginning, was smiling now. "Come up behind me, boy," he said. "I will take you both, and gladly."

"No, a trade!" Ulf insisted. "You know I am the better choice, and I will be the better traveler. This one still cries at night for his mother, I think." He remembered that, too.

The little boy made a face. His mouth moved. "No, I don't!" it said.

The rider's frown returned. "*They* won't be taking care of him anymore," he said, pointing to the watchman and his son. "It seems a waste to leave him here by himself, for the wolves."

Ulf took a careful breath. "That dog knows where his mother lives," he said. "The dog could take him home."

The little boy smiled at last, but the warrior who held the dog shook his head. "Not this dog!" he said. "She's my battle prize, and I'll keep her."

Ulf's teeth pressed his lip so hard that he tasted blood. His head was buzzing, but nothing clever came into it. He could think of no argument that would free the dog.

"He—he could find his own way home," Ulf stammered. "It's only just back over this path, here." He said these words as clearly as he could, hoping the boy would know, somehow, that he should go there, that someone was waiting. But the child was looking at the dog, chin trembling, and he began to sob.

"None of that!" the rider said. "Get on down, then!" And he lifted Jeremy's brother off the horse's back and plopped him in the tall brown grass at the edge of the trees. "You're right," he said to Ulf. "It's best to leave him. Look at this odd stuff he wears. Could be a wizard's child."

Then the man inched forward on his horse to make room for Ulf, swung him up with one arm, and trotted toward the warriors who still milled about, shouting and claiming prisoners, along the wall of the keep. The foot soldier tagged after, pulling the dog, who stopped every few paces to look back at the child in the grass and whine.

Ulf's spirit was heavy as lead. Here was a day that promised to make truth of all his dreams—to bring him escape from this place and its punishments and to keep him near to Gudrun the Fair. Even Magic, the companion of his heart, was close at hand. Yet that was not where the dog needed to be, and it made everything wrong. The sun was up, the queen was dead. It was a day made for rejoicing, but Ulf could not rejoice. If Magic went to the north with any of Gudrun's people, how could Jeremy and the others ever get back to their homes? He did not even dare to imagine what the wizard might say.

CHAPTER 12

❖ *Jeremy*

"Jeremy! Jeremy! Where you been?" Sniffles and sobs rose up out of the weeds.

"Austin! Shhh! Austin, it's all right." Jeremy crouched to fold his little brother in a hug. "You're a big guy, remember? Shhh." For a moment, Jeremy was so happy to have found him, to be with him, that he couldn't remember one thing Austin had ever done to annoy him.

"What about you, Quinn?" he asked over Austin's shoulder. "Are you feeling okay now?" He had felt like cheering when Quinn volunteered to bean Austin's kidnapper with a rock.

Quinn was staying low in the long grass, peering after the men who made their way toward the walled stone building across the meadow. "Better, I guess. Not okay, exactly. It helps to be out in the air like this, with the sun and all, and just you guys. But it's still way too weird, Jeremy," he said. "I don't get it."

Jeremy sighed. "Me, either." He thought of the story Ulf had told them, how there were bits and pieces of it in his mother's papers, but he didn't know what that could mean. He had to remember to ask Quinn about it when he was all the way better. But at least Quinn seemed more like himself now, like someone he could talk to. Maybe he wasn't ready to be in charge just yet, but certainly he could help. Jeremy allowed himself one little moment of relief before he went on to the next thing, to the huge, enormous, gigantic problem of the dog. "Can you still see Duchess?" he said to Quinn.

Quinn shook his head. "Grass is too high. And I can't tell which of those foot soldiers had her, either. From this distance they all look the same."

"Except for the ones that aren't getting up," Jeremy said with a shudder. He thought about the battle board in Quinn's basement and how they scattered warriors across it and picked them up and did it all over again. And then he looked toward the crumpled men on the ground near the wall, and for a moment, although he didn't know exactly why, he thought he was going to double up and cry, just the way Austin was doing.

"I want Richelle," Austin said against Jeremy's shoulder.

Jeremy took a breath. "Later, okay?"

Austin snuffled. "Where *is* Richelle?"

Jeremy sighed. He supposed he could find where the wizard lived, but he wasn't absolutely certain. He thought with gratitude of Ulf, who had convinced the horseman to let Austin go, but he wished Ulf could have stayed with them. What if they couldn't get back to Richelle without his help?

Jeremy wiped Austin's tears with the palm of his hand. "We have to go after Duchess before we can see Richelle," he said. "We have to get our dog back. Okay?"

Austin nodded.

"What do we do?" Quinn said. "Are we just going over there and whistle for her, or what?"

Jeremy frowned. He had hoped Quinn would come up with a better idea than that. "No," he said, trying to think fast. "We can't see her right now, and it doesn't look very safe over there, all out in the open like that." Not to mention the fallen men and the horses that were either dead or dying. Jeremy didn't think he wanted to be any closer than he was already.

"Maybe there's a better place for getting Duchess back," he said, as things began to sort themselves out in his mind. "That guy who took her probably wants to take her home with him, right? And they all got here in boats or something, didn't they? Isn't that what Ulf said? And we heard them in the ravine as they came in, so—"

"Right." Quinn took up the thought. "They'll probably go back that way, to wherever the boats are."

Jeremy nodded. "So we need to get back to the path we were on before daylight and go down to the ravine and follow the stream and—" Ms. Hernandez would have been proud of his logic, he thought as they started out, Austin trudging between them.

Although the way was easier in daylight, the going took longer than Jeremy expected. They had to stop once to rest and twice to figure out which way to go. Where the footing was solid enough, they carried Austin, taking turns. By the time they had climbed down the bank to the stream, they were tired and thirsty beyond anything Jeremy had ever imagined. He studied the water running along over rocks, bubbling clear in the sun.

"I suppose we shouldn't drink it," he said, lowering his voice for only Quinn to hear. "What if we turn into toads or something? Or get terrible germs?"

Quinn twisted one side of his mouth. "You sound just like Richelle," he said.

In the end, Jeremy's throat was too dry for him to resist. They all got down on their knees, put their faces to the water, and drank. It made Jeremy remember how Duchess stood over her bowl at home, and he thought again how much they missed and needed her. "We'd better hurry up," he said.

When they heard voices somewhere on the bank above them, they left the path along the stream to make their way around trees and through the cover of the thickets.

"How much longer?" Austin said again and again as the sun rolled into afternoon. "I'm hungry. I want to go home."

"Please don't whine, Austin," Jeremy said. He was afraid the sound of that sad little voice would make him too discouraged to go on. But all at once he had an inspiration. With both hands he dug into his jacket and brought out the tiny ancient warriors. "Look what you can have if you'll be quiet," he said. He didn't think he would ever again want them for his own.

"Okay!" Austin took the figures greedily into his own pockets, keeping two to hold, one for each hand. When he smiled with his lips pressed together, Jeremy knew he understood his part of the bargain.

In the quiet that followed, Quinn tugged at Jeremy's sleeve. "Don't you think we're lost?" he hissed. "There's no place here with enough water for a ship. Maybe there's a fork in this stream and we missed it."

Jeremy didn't see how that was possible, but he worried anyway. It was a great relief to come to the broad path that the warriors had used, with its scuffle of footprints and the marks of many horses. After that they were extra cautious, although no sentry appeared to question their slow progress downstream. The ravine grew wider, the embankments lower. They rounded a bend, and then, with one more step, they could see the place where the stream emptied into a broad river.

A line of ships, six of them, rode at anchor far out in the water. Jeremy caught his breath. The markings on their sails were as fierce in shape and color as anything he had ever seen on a video screen. Worse, really. The wind that puffed and fell against them made them seem to breathe. "Wow," said Austin, and Jeremy put a quick finger to his lips. A small troop of men with swords and shields stood guard along the river. A few others were clustered on a broad, flat stone at the water's edge. Near it, several small boats were drawn up against the bank.

"They're cleaning their weapons," Quinn whispered. "Look at those swords!"

Jeremy blinked to wipe away his memory of how the weapons came to need cleaning in the first place.

"Come on," he said to Quinn, pulling Austin back a few steps farther from the stream, into a clump of bushes thick enough to hide them all. Jeremy tried to concentrate. They would have to make a plan now, he thought—how to watch for Duchess and then keep her in sight, how to snatch her away from her captor, how to get back to Richelle. . . . He opened his mouth to ask Quinn what he thought, in spite of Quinn's white face. But as it turned out, there was no time for planning.

All of a sudden, the guards on the shore set up a shout, and there were answering cries far back along the path. And then it seemed the whole ravine came alive with warriors and horses, with yelling and wild singing, drums beating, horns blaring. Some of the men came crashing by almost near enough to touch, dangerously close to their hiding place. Jeremy had never heard or seen anything as powerful or as loud or as strange to him as this triumphant army coming back to the river. He felt Austin's hand come creeping into his own.

"What if we can't ever find Duchess in all this mess?" Quinn whispered when the worst of the noise had moved beyond them and only stragglers passed along the path. "What if we can't go home?"

Jeremy put a warning hand on his arm. Much as it worried him, he didn't want to talk about that possibility where Austin could hear.

But Austin was paying the bigger boys no attention. "Listen," he said. "Listen, guys! I hear Duchess!"

Jeremy held his breath. He hadn't seen a dog anywhere, yet from the midst of the pandemonium near the river came the unmistakable sound of barking. He crept just beyond the edge of their shelter for a better look. Swordsmen, archers, and horsemen were all scattered about along the river near the mouth of the stream. One of the big ships had maneuvered close to the shore, and brawny men with yellow beards pushed huge planks out over the side and onto the bank. Horses whinnied shrill complaints as they were coaxed up to the deck. Two of the little boats carried warriors toward the ships that waited far out in the water.

It was hard to see much at all without the fear of being seen. Jeremy despaired of being able to pick out a dog—one that was no longer barking—in the midst of so much confusion. He searched everywhere with his eyes, scanning first the bank and then the men who stood and sat in the back rank, nearer to the boys. They were lean men, their arms and legs knotted with muscle. He marveled at how dirty and unkempt they were and at their rough weapons, still dark with the terrible filth of battle. Here and there a man groaned or held a fist against some stain on his tunic. It was a good thing Richelle wasn't here, Jeremy thought. Or his mother. A sudden image of home came washing over him like a wave, leaving him breathless. What if Quinn was right? What if they couldn't get back? Where was Duchess?

"There she is!" Quinn said from behind him, as if he had asked his question aloud.

Jeremy's eyes sighted along his friend's pointing finger to the river's edge. The warrior who had taken the dog from the huge man in the woods now struggled to carry her, big as she was, toward one of the small boats. It would soon have a full load, Jeremy saw. If Duchess got taken out to one of the ships, how would they ever get her back? His heart pounded.

"Stay here and take care of the little warriors, Austin." The words came tumbling out. "And Quinn, you keep him out of the way here. Make sure he's safe." He turned to glance once at Quinn's horrified expression, and then he bolted out of their hiding place and went running through the jumble of armed men toward the river.

"That's my dog!" he shouted. "Give her back!" Taken by surprise, men stepped out of his path, making room. If he had thought about their weapons, about their strength, he would have been terrified. But all his focus was on the dog. The only thing he saw clearly was how Duchess thrashed in the man's arms. At last she jumped and landed on her feet, although she was tethered to the warrior by the strap that still encircled her neck. She barked and waggled her entire backside as if Jeremy were just coming home from school.

"Duchess!" he panted. He was almost close enough to touch her now. "Good girl! Let's go home!" He reached for the strap because he didn't know any other way to claim her. "She's mine," he said, but unlike Ulf and the wizard, the man who held Duchess didn't seem to understand the words. He held the strap out of Jeremy's reach. Panting, Jeremy pointed his finger at the dog and then at his own chest.

The warrior regarded him with suspicious eyes. Jeremy

took one small step toward Duchess. In less than a second, the man moved in front of the dog. He shouted and drew a short blade out of the sash he wore low on his tunic. He shouted again, and slashed. Jeremy tried to move out of the way, but he felt the sting and saw the thin thread of blood near his wrist before he even had a good look at the weapon, and then he was too terrified to cry out. Duchess was trying to bark, but her captor had twisted her neck-piece so that she could only cough. She tried to snap at him, but he had wound the strap so many times around his hand that the dog's teeth could not reach him.

Jeremy heard his own heartbeat in the silence that had fallen around him as men gathered to watch. He took a step backward, breathing hard, trying to think how to defend himself. But in the next instant, the warrior leaped forward and pressed his blade flat against Jeremy's chest, its tip under his chin. Jeremy tried to stand still, to look brave, but no amount of effort could stop his body from shaking. He thought all at once of Mr. DaSilva's beautiful dagger, safely out of reach in its scabbard under Quinn's jacket. A lot of good it was doing them there! He gritted his teeth and hoped for a miracle.

CHAPTER 13

❖ Ulf

Ulf's fingers rested on the leather cuff that marked him now as taken for service, but his eyes were on the river. His warrior guardian had judged him at no risk of running away and had sent him alone to watch for the small boat with a sun carved into its side. It would take them to one of the great ships, which would carry them down to the sea and then north to Gudrun's homeland and her marriage feast. There, so Ulf was told, he would be among the tributes offered to the bride by Prince Orton's men. He would be bound to the princess, to serve her at Zirn and wherever else her life might take her. The whole idea was more than Ulf had dreamed—to be on the water, traveling far; to stay always near to Gudrun, who had been a friend to him; to be part of a household where he would not be scorned for an outlander. But he could only be happy for a few moments at a time. His mind kept returning to Magic and to his last night's companions. If they did not find her and go safely back to their own land, there would be danger here and everywhere. The wizard himself had said it.

And so Ulf's eyes were on the bank more than on the water, watching for the dog instead of the little boat. He longed to set her free. If he could do even that much, she might find the others on her own. She was a good dog, and loyal. He was sorry still that she could not be his.

He watched as the hawk watches, but at last it was his ears and not his eyes that rewarded him. He heard barking, and even though it did not continue, he hurried in the direction of the sound. Ulf slipped in and out among the men crowded near the washing stone, avoiding the turmoil of horses waiting to be taken on board ship. When he heard the dog again, her tone had changed, and he began to run. At last he pushed his way through a ring of men who stood muttering at the water's edge.

Ulf gasped. In the middle of the space was the foot soldier who had claimed Magic that morning. He still had her, one hand twisting the strap to tighten it on her neck, the other gripping a sword with a short blade. And at that moment he was holding the weapon flat against the chest of a boy with no color in his face. It was Jeremy.

"No!" cried Ulf, searching for words because he had no weapon. "You—you dare not hurt that boy!"

The warrior laughed. "Stop me, then, little slave," he said.

Ulf saw Jeremy's eyes flicker toward him and then to the dog in a plea that he understood but could not acknowledge.

"Listen," he said to the man, and words began to come to him. "Can't you see he's a wizard's boy?" The warrior blinked once.

"Look at what he wears!" Ulf went on. "Look at his feet! Nothing but magic would make shoes curve around the heel and toe like that." Ulf began to hear murmuring from the men who were gathered around. "Look at the front of that covering he wears, that strange tunic. See the tiny piece of shiny stuff at the top? He pulls that down, and the garment splits in two. He pulls it up, and the two parts become one again—all by wizardry, I tell you."

The soldier let his eyes slide up and down Jeremy's chest, and then he moved his hand, blade and all, to try that magic for himself. Poor Jeremy, Ulf thought.

"Best you not touch those garments," Ulf warned quickly. "Best not to be that close. You should leave a wizard's boy alone. No telling what ill fortune you bring yourself by sticking that blade into him."

All around the circle, men drew breath sharply, making the sign against evil. The warrior, too, was convinced. He pushed Jeremy away with such force that the boy fell in a heap at Ulf's feet. "Go!" the man shouted as the dog whined and pawed at the ground beside him. "Go, and take your enchantments with you!" He waved the weapon over his head.

Jeremy took the hand that Ulf offered him and pulled himself slowly upright to face the warrior. "I won't go without my dog," he said. The words were firm, but the voice squeaked. He pointed to her and held out his hand for the leash.

Ulf saw a drop of blood fall from the wound above Jeremy's wrist. His breath came faster. "Send the wizard's dog away now with the boy," he said urgently to the warrior, who had begun to curse at Jeremy for his disobedience.

"Magic dogs are no end of trouble," Ulf continued. "If you doubt what she is, look at her eyes. Those are no dog's eyes. There's wolf in them, see?" A few of the watchers moved in for a better view, and it seemed to Ulf that Magic drew herself up to stand straighter in spite of the indignity of her tether.

"And this coat!" Ulf went on. "Who but a wizard would have a dog with hair as long as this? Or as bright? Who knows where she might go or what she might be hunting when your back is turned?"

The dog's captor frowned at that and turned himself a little to look at his prize, although he kept the strap wound securely on his hand. He glanced around once at Ulf, and then twice.

"I know you, boy!" he shouted suddenly. "You and your tricks! I saw you this morning, talking your way up onto the captain's horse." He took a step toward Ulf. "You already tried once this morning to get this dog away from me. You didn't call it a wizard's dog then. I remember, boy. You lie! This dog is mine!" He pointed his knife at Jeremy. "I have no use for this one," he said, "but the dog goes with me!"

Ulf caught Jeremy's eye and saw there was no need to explain the warrior's words. The man's intent was clear. Both boys looked toward the dog, who was growling, deep in her throat, in answer to the latest tug at her neck. Then, as if they had planned together, Jeremy lunged for the dog's strap while Ulf threw himself toward the one who held her.

This man was trained for warfare, Ulf knew, but even so he had not bargained for such great speed. The warrior whirled out of the boy's reach and turned back to him at once with his weapon raised to strike. Ulf held up his arms to ward off the blow and closed his eyes against it. Here was the end, he thought. He hoped the wizard would know how hard he had tried to make right the trouble he had caused by coveting this dog.

And in that same instant, in the very moment he expected his own death, he heard someone scream his name instead: "Ulf! Ulf Who Carries Water!" The dog began to bark amid a chorus of shouts and cries. The boy's eyes flew open to behold at his side the princess Gudrun, on horseback, using the end of one rein to flog the shoulders of the warrior who threatened him. Jeremy was on his knees beside the dog, hugging her, holding her back, quieting her. Ulf's mouth gaped open, and his breath began to come in and out again, as it should.

The circle of watchers fell back to make room for Prince Orton and Prince Erik of Zirn, who came walking beside their mounts, laughing. "Enough, my sister," the one said. "This fellow will know better than to mistreat any of your favorites again." Orton spoke a command, and the warrior went slinking away, leaving the dog behind.

The princess was calmer now, although her face was very pink and the gown she wore, green as summer and fit for a royal wedding, was askew. She gestured to Erik, and he handed her down from her mount.

"I thought you were to stay safely hidden today, Ulf," Gudrun said softly.

He blushed and dropped his head in apology.

"But I see your beautiful dog has come to you again," she went on, as if that explained everything.

"I was mistaken, my lady," he said, and he swallowed. "She is not my dog, or even the wizard's." He pointed to Jeremy. "She has a home already, and Harket says she— *they*—must go back to it."

Gudrun's eyes flashed wide. She looked from Ulf to Jeremy. "Where under the great sun—" she began, and stopped. At last she turned back to Ulf. "What help is needed?" she said.

Ulf's spirit swelled with gratitude. "Safe passage through these troops and up the stream to the wizard's hut, I think. Nothing more. Thank you, my lady."

"It is soon done," she said, and smiled and spoke behind her hand to her brother. "The sentries will watch after them all the way. Will you go with them, Ulf?" she asked as Prince Orton turned to one of his men.

Ulf shook his head. "I am a battle prize," he whispered. "I am to be taken to your homeland as a wedding gift for you." He could not hold back the smile that came to him and nearly split his face.

"Ulf!" cried the girl in a voice as pleased as his own. "Oh, Ulf, I am happy! You *are* a prize!" And Princess Gudrun's laughter, sweet and clear, rang out over the very place where she had labored as a washerwoman just the day before. She touched Ulf's shoulder. Then, with Prince Erik, she moved on toward the journey that would restore her to the life she had lost.

For a while Ulf stared after her, wondering how he would spend his days in that new homeland, considering the chance of more loneliness in store for him there. He shuddered without meaning to. Then his mind came back to the present, and he hurried to crouch beside Jeremy and the dog. He let his hand rest on Magic's silky fur, touching the tangles that marred it now. He looked deep into the gray of her eyes and down the white of her chest, noticing for the first time the golden speckles just above her feet. Ulf studied the look and feel of her and put it in his memory to stay. "Magic," he said softly and fondled her ears while her tail swung happily side to side. It was harder to take leave of her than he had thought.

Jeremy cleared his throat. "I don't know exactly how you did it," he said, "but thanks. It's—it's great, what you did for Austin and me, and for Duchess. Could I give you, like—a present, or something? Would you like to have this jacket, with the zipper?"

Ulf shook his head. There was only one thing of Jeremy's that he desired, and he knew he could not have it. "You have safe passage back to the wizard," Ulf said slowly, making himself stand and look away from the dog. "Just follow the stream, and you'll see the way to his hut. Tell Harket our story, and say I am gone away to serve Gudrun the Fair. Please."

Jeremy nodded and thanked him again.

Ulf tried to swallow the lump in his throat. "It is best you should hurry," he said. "Hurry and don't look back." Slowly Ulf turned toward the river, not watching them go. He wondered how it was that his heart could be so heavy, just when so many good things had happened.

❖ *Jeremy*

Jeremy was too exhausted to run, but he hurried as best he could, stumbling along with his tender wrist against his middle. Duchess trotted at his other side, still at the end of the strap that had made her a prisoner. He didn't think he could untie the knots in it, and anyway, it made him feel more secure to be connected to her even though they made their way without any trouble among the warriors.

Jeremy felt more at ease when they had moved beyond the crowd, but then, fuzzy-brained, he could not pick out the place where he had left Quinn and his little brother. All the bushes and thickets along the stream were alike to his tired eyes. He stopped to look for something, anything, that seemed familiar. Terrible thoughts came crowding into his mind. What if someone else had found them? Had taken them away? Had done them harm? Duchess sat at his feet, head cocked, one ear up and one ear down. She whined softly.

Jeremy let out a long breath. How simple can I be? he thought suddenly, and he rubbed Duchess's floppy ear and whispered in it. "Let's go get Austin," he said to her. "Let's find Quinn!" They set out on a zigzag course, going from the path toward the bank of the ravine and back again. In practically no time Duchess had stopped at a clump of bushes and refused to go farther, thrusting herself deep into the tangle. When her tail began to swing furiously, Jeremy plowed in beside her. There was Quinn, sitting in a hollow among the branches, his legs folded to make a space in which Austin was curled, fast asleep. Quinn's own neck was bent, his head nodding.

"Guys!" said Jeremy. "Wake up! Come on!" Duchess moved closer to slurp first one face and then the other.

"What?" Quinn sputtered. "Hey, great! Are you two okay? I couldn't see one thing from in here."

Austin's eyes flew open. "It's Duchess!" he squealed, but it was Jeremy he reached for. Jeremy gave his little brother a happy squeeze. He felt that maybe now he should pinch himself. They were almost all together again. Who would have believed it?

Quinn patted Duchess and smiled one of his regular, everyday smiles, the first Jeremy had seen in a long time. "Richelle will be having a cow," Quinn said, separating himself from Austin and the dog. "Let's go! Come on!"

Jeremy smiled back. It felt great to be hopeful again. The return of good spirits was even bringing his energy back. He wasn't tired anymore, and the pain in his wrist had faded. Who had time to think about such trivial stuff? The important thing was, he and Quinn and Austin and the dog were finally in the same place at the same time. All they had to do now was get Richelle, and then they could go home.

It was beginning to seem easy. They came out into the open and started up through the ravine, beyond the broad track the warriors had taken and on into the narrows, where the banks were steeper. Jeremy kept Duchess close. Who knew if there might be squirrels? Austin ran a little way ahead, turning every half minute to call to them— "This way, guys! This is the path!"

Jeremy didn't even tell him to be quiet. He was using all his breath to explain to Quinn what had happened at the river, especially the part about the girl on horseback who had saved Ulf. "You should have seen it," he said. "It was great. She's the princess Ulf told us about last night, I guess, the one named Gudrun. He said there were two princes who wanted to marry her, but I can hardly believe it. I don't think she was any older than Richelle. Can you think of anyone who would want to marry Richelle? Huh?" The very idea made Jeremy laugh.

Quinn shrugged. "You remember those eighth graders who wanted me to play ball with them?" He made a sour face. "They didn't care if I'd ever seen a football before. What they really wanted was for me to fix it so they could meet my sister."

"No kidding!" Jeremy would have said more, but just then they heard Austin shouting Richelle's name. They all began to run.

She was sitting on a rock at the end of a narrow path that led away from the stream. Jeremy supposed it must be the path to the wizard's little house, but it disappeared so quickly that he wondered if he would have found it without Richelle for a signpost. She got to her feet and began to hurry toward them. Jeremy was relieved to see that she was hardly limping at all. Maybe she would be able to climb the bank and go home under her own power.

Austin ran straight into the girl's arms, and she babbled over him just like the Richelle that Jeremy had always known. "Quinn! Jeremy!" She tried to hug them, too, but Jeremy managed to wiggle away. "I've been *so* worried. You don't *know* how worried I've been! And—oh, poor Duchess! Just look at your coat!"

Jeremy opened his mouth to tell her that he needed to talk to the wizard, but Richelle wasn't listening. "Come on now, all of you," she said. "We aren't waiting another minute. We have to go *home*. Jeremy, don't you let this dog get away!"

Jeremy frowned. "I'm supposed to deliver a message to the wizard first—a message from Ulf."

"Oh, come on, Jeremy, please!" Richelle said. "Let him deliver his own messages. Those old people are creepy! I can't wait to get out of here. They don't have a bathroom or anything! It's so—"

"Yeah, Jeremy, why don't we go?" Quinn broke in. He was looking nervous again. "We're all here now, and the longer we wait, the more chance there is for something else weird to happen."

"I want to go home now, too," said Austin. "Right now! I'm *hungry.* I want to see *cartoons.*"

"We don't even know what time it is at home," Richelle said. "Maybe Dad's off work by now."

Quinn looked anxiously from one bank of the ravine to the other. "Yeah, Jeremy," he said. "Come *on!*"

Austin left Richelle's side and came to his brother, hugging him around the waist. "Pleeease!" he said softly. "Let's go *now*."

"I'm the oldest," Richelle said, "and I'm in charge, and I say we go." She glared at Jeremy.

"Okay, okay." He sighed, looping the dog's strap around itself and tucking it under the piece that circled her neck, hoping she wouldn't snare herself in the brush. "Let's go on up, Duchess," he said, and he held his hands out to her to show her she was free. "Let's go home, girl. You're the one who knows the way."

The dog made her own path. She led them around bare trees and half-bare thickets, over fallen branches, and through weeds that clutched at their clothes. "Take it easy, girl," Jeremy said to check her speed. Austin needed help most of the time, and Richelle was slow, too, favoring her ankle and studying every step.

"There might be snakes," she said.

Quinn had gone on ahead of the dog. "Almost there!" he called.

"Stay together," Jeremy reminded them. "We should all be with Duchess, I think." Anticipation filled him like a balloon. He wondered if the others felt the same—as if they could float upward those last few steps.

Quinn boosted Austin over the edge just as Duchess scrambled up. Jeremy reached back to give Richelle a hand, and when he turned, all he could do was blink.

"Where's the sidewalk?" Austin demanded. "*This* isn't home!"

Richelle buried her face in her hands.

Jeremy stared from side to side. To their right, the lip of the ravine disappeared into a forest that stretched on and on and up and up, ending on a mountaintop. The trees in front of them were sparse enough to let them glimpse a bit of meadow and a corner of orchard. Far to the left was a great, rambling structure of stone with a wall that went on out of sight.

"We were right over there this morning," Quinn breathed. "We're still *here*! We didn't go *anywhere*!"

Duchess sat without being told. Her tail was perfectly still. They were all quiet for a time, even Austin, although his chin quivered.

Jeremy tried to think, but nothing made sense. "I just don't understand it," he said finally. "I guess the only thing we can do now is go back to the wizard."

No one argued. They made their way slowly back down the bank, not having the heart to talk, and presented themselves at the door of the little hut.

CHAPTER 14

❖ *Jeremy*

"But it *should* work," Jeremy said earnestly to Harket. He had carefully explained everything he could about their earlier search and what had happened to Ulf and their failed attempt at going home. "I don't understand why Duchess couldn't take us home this time," he said. "It worked once when Quinn and I came by accident, and it worked again when I tried it out by myself. I just can't figure it out."

"Many things are beyond our figuring, boy," the wizard said, in a voice that sent prickles up and down Jeremy's neck. Harket turned his eyes to the little fire on the hearth, and Duchess left her spot beside the door to lie at the old man's feet. He stroked her head, and Jeremy wondered if his dog could feel the same tingling he had felt at the wizard's touch.

Jeremy and Quinn and Austin and Richelle were squeezed together at the crude benches that flanked the table, where the wizard's wife set a basket with chunks of dark, flat bread. Jeremy's stomach was so pinched and empty that he overcame his caution and took a piece. But as he reached for it, his sleeve crept up and showed the mark near his wrist that was smeared with dry blood.

"Ooh," whispered Richelle. "Are you all right, Jeremy? When did you do that?"

"Today," he mumbled, chewing hard. He didn't bother to tell more. There were some things that Richelle and Austin didn't ever need to know, he thought, because when they got home, they would tell his mother for sure.

"Jeremy," Richelle began, but just then the wizard cleared his throat and brought his eyes back to the group at the table, commanding everyone's attention. Austin wiggled into Richelle's lap and hid his face against her.

"Your dog came through a slip between our two worlds," Harket said without preface, "a passageway from your time and place into ours." His voice was grave. "The boy Ulf, the one who helped you, was lonely and longed for a dog, and his need called to her. But now that he is leaving—" The wizard paused. "Although his longing is the same, his need is less."

Harket paused again, and Jeremy's memory flashed him

a picture of Ulf saying good-bye to Duchess. Much as he hated the idea of anyone else claiming his dog, he felt a little rush of sympathy. If Ulf liked her so much, that must have been hard.

"And now that the boy's need is less," continued the wizard, "the slip—the passageway—may be fading."

"What?" said Jeremy. He looked from Quinn to Richelle, seeing how his own shock was reflected in both their faces. "You mean if that passageway is gone, we might not ever get home? Even with Duchess to guide us?" The dog sat up at the mention of her name.

"There is that chance," the wizard said. His wife moved to lay a handful of sticks on the fire. Jeremy's nose twitched at the new scent.

"Can't we do anything about it?" Quinn asked. His eyes were round as quarters.

"If the slip fades," Harket said gently, "if there is no place of connection, there is no way to return."

Jeremy rubbed his forehead. "Could you, like, maybe make another connection, Mr. Harket, sir?"

The old man's eyes rested on him like a weight. "Our worlds touch as they will, boy," the wizard said sternly. "Some things cannot be had for the wanting. There is no magic in this land to call up that connection."

Jeremy couldn't bear to think it. "Maybe we're still connected a little bit," he said. "Could that be?"

Harket nodded slowly. "Perhaps," he said, "because the

tie was strong, and the slip was wide. The dog came and went many times. I was even able to pass through, myself."

The old woman looked quickly at her husband. The word *prowler* came into Jeremy's mind and into Quinn's and Richelle's, too, he guessed, judging from their expressions.

"I have thought that it took more than one boy and one dog to open such a way and keep it clear," the wizard continued. "Something else, some circumstance in your world, may have chanced to happen at the same time, holding us close. It might be there still, keeping the way open."

"Could it be our ravine?" asked Richelle. "I mean, it's not exactly like this one, but it's sort of similar, and it's right in our neighborhood, and the boys went there to play sometimes even though they weren't supposed to." Jeremy and Quinn exchanged guilty glances, avoiding the wizard's eyes.

"That is no small matter," said Harket, nodding toward the girl. "Ravines are hidden places where water runs, erasing secrets. One ravine slips easily into another. Open fields are much less likely." He rubbed the dog's neck. "But place alone cannot explain an entrapment," he said. "Something else has tied us together."

"Ancient warriors!" said Quinn suddenly. He swallowed and opened his mouth as if to speak again, but no more words came out.

Harket's bristling white eyebrows drew together in puzzlement.

"The warriors that we played with in the ravine," Jeremy said as explanation. "You know, just little model soldiers. Miniatures." The old man frowned. "Toys!" said Jeremy, and then the wizard sighed.

"Tell me," Harket directed, and so the two boys took turns describing their games. They told him how their warriors moved by the chance of the dice or just for the fun of it, at the players' whim, sometimes on the battle board, sometimes over mosses and stones in the ravine.

"One thing, though," Jeremy said, "and I don't know if Quinn feels this way or if it's just me." He looked at his friend. "It seemed like more fun when I was home than it does to me now. Those little warriors don't bleed like real ones do, or swing their weapons around, trying to hurt you. And they don't stay dead, you know? It was pretty ugly today, I thought."

Quinn nodded, and across the table, Richelle's face showed her dismay. "What have you two been *doing*?" she said, but the boys paid her no attention. Jeremy's eyes were on the wizard and on his wife, who had come to his side and was whispering against the old man's ear.

"Yes," murmured Harket, and "yes" again, nodding, and then he sat straighter and looked at the boys. "Where are these little figures now?" he asked.

"At home," said Quinn.

"Well, most of them," corrected Jeremy. "I had some in my pocket when we came here and I gave them to my brother to play with, to keep him quiet. Show him, Austin. Show him what they look like."

"Yes," said the wizard. "Perhaps, if Berta could just hold them in her hand. . . ."

Austin clutched Richelle and buried his head in the crook of her arm. "No," he said, "I can't do it." His voice was muffled.

"Don't be afraid," Jeremy coaxed.

"I can't do it," Austin repeated, and he looked up, ready to cry. "The little soldiers are way back there where we were walking. They're in the water, hiding from those big guys on their horses."

"Oh, no," said Jeremy. "Every one of them? Are you sure? Stand up and pat your pockets, like this." As he showed Austin what to do, his own fingers found a bump deep under his zippered sweatshirt. Frantically he put his left hand in the left pocket and drew out one lone forgotten warrior, a pewter figure mounted on a pewter horse, with stiff little battle ribbons marking him as royalty. It was the figure that most reminded Jeremy of the rider he and Quinn had seen in the ravine that first time.

The wizard's wife made a sound of warning in her throat. "Armut," she whispered, and shook her head.

"Take good care," Harket said, very low. "Use a soft touch when you put it in her hand, boy."

What's going on? Jeremy thought, and little tickles of fear began to circle his collar. Carefully he laid the warrior on Berta's palm.

"Could this be our connection, maybe?" he asked. "Could this take us home?"

"No, child." The old woman spoke but did not offer to return the figure to him. Instead, she plucked a jar from the shelf behind her, popped the warrior into it, and stoppered it tightly. "Such things might have helped to bring you here," she said, "but they cannot take you back."

"No!" Richelle cried. "How can that be right? That's not fair!" Then Austin began to wail, and Jeremy took him from Richelle and into his own lap.

"Try to understand, children," the wizard said. "In our world, such figures are not used for play, but for the transfer of great power. Danger follows them."

Jeremy bit his lip, wondering what harm he might have brought to his little brother by giving him the warriors to carry.

"Unfortunately," Harket went on, "the power can be used only to"—he hesitated—"only to make things wrong, not to make them right again."

"We should get rid of all our ancient warriors, then, shouldn't we?" asked Jeremy. He looked at Quinn, who sat silent, his jaw slack.

The wizard shrugged. "In your world, perhaps there is no harm."

"But I wouldn't want to take any chances," Jeremy said.

"Oh, Jeremy," Quinn said, "stop kidding yourself! There won't be any chances to take, because we aren't ever going to be able to get back. We're going to be stuck forever in some old place just like the one your mother was writing about."

"Quinn!" Jeremy cried, letting Austin slide onto the bench beside him. "You're a genius! That's a connection!" He took a giant breath. "Listen, Mr. Harket, sir," he said, "there's this one other thing, this story—"

"Yeah, his mother is writing it," Quinn put in, picking up his friend's enthusiasm.

Jeremy shook his head. "No, not exactly. It's already written down in lots of different books and even different languages. She's just, like, telling it over again."

"We read a little bit of it," Quinn said, "where one old king named Ludwig fights another one 'to the death.' "

"And see," Jeremy continued, "then Ulf told us about the princess Gudrun and how her father was killed and how the queen here was so mean to her, and the story has something just like that."

"Jeremy!" said Richelle. "Are you making all this up?"

"No," said Jeremy. "I'm not. Honest, Richelle, the story my mother was working on is so much like here you wouldn't believe it. Haven't you seen her books and junk all over the house? Stuff about weapons and Northern legends and that book called *Gudrun's Tale* that she's always losing?" Richelle pinched up her face to think about it.

Harket the wizard was leaning forward in his seat. "A story, you say?"

"Yes, sir."

"Who is to hear it?"

"Anyone who wants to read it, I guess. It's—" Jeremy considered explaining how his mother wrote at the computer and could send her words almost anywhere, but that seemed too complicated, too magical. He swallowed and started over. "It's—you know—words on paper, or it will be, and it's going into a book, and then—"

"Yes." Harket pressed one hand to his temple. "Words in a book . . . Yes." He looked up at Jeremy, suddenly intent. "This tale that she tells—is it finished?"

"I—I don't think so," Jeremy told him. "Almost, though. She needed just a little more time, she said."

The wizard nodded gravely. "Then something of the slip remains," he said. "It began with the dog, and your game brought you into it. And now, as long as someone close to you still tries to snare our world with words, we cannot escape the connection. The telling of the story, that is our entrapment." He shook his head sadly.

"But then we *can* go home!" Richelle cried, and she started to get up. "If we hurry!"

The old man coughed and shifted in his seat. "Have

patience," he said. "Remember that you have tried once to pass through, and failed."

Quinn smacked the table with one open hand. "I don't see what good it does to have a slip or whatever unless we can get through it," he said.

"Why *can't* we go home?" Austin asked into the silence. "Huh, Jeremy? I want Mommy now."

Jeremy gave Austin a hug. They couldn't just give up.

"Mr. Harket, sir," he said, "can you give us any help at all? Do you know why we can't go through the slip?"

The wizard looked into the fire. "A slip is still there, and yet it was closed to you," he said. "In the old rules of wizardry, it is said that travelers who come through a slip may not return if they have stayed too long."

"How long is too long?" Jeremy's mouth was deadly dry. "How were we supposed to know?"

Harket shrugged. "Wizards talk of such things when they meet," he said, "but they have no answer."

Jeremy heard Richelle take a long breath. "What can we do?" she begged. "Can't we do *something*?"

"Berta?" the old man said. "What do you think?"

The old woman looked at the children one by one, and her face was kindly. "There is a saying," she told them, "and it is this: 'They go through the slip who leave something of value behind. They go, who leave something, or someone, behind.'" She was whispering now. "So it is said."

Jeremy felt suddenly empty, absolutely hopeless. Richelle and Quinn felt it, too, he could tell. They all shifted in their seats, leaning toward one another. Even Duchess left the wizard's feet and came to lie by theirs.

"That's—that's outrageous!" Richelle was the one who finally spoke, wiping at her eyes. "We can't just some of us go," she said. "It has to be all of us. And you *know* we aren't going to have anything of value—not here with us, anyway."

"Well, we do have *something* valuable," Jeremy protested. "You know, there's friendship and stuff like that." He shrugged. "But we wouldn't want to go and leave that behind, even if we knew how."

"The rules are harsh, child," Berta agreed, "but not of our own making. We must live by them, too."

"Far better for us if we could send you home to your families," the wizard said. "Great trouble may follow you here. Even if it does not, it will be hard for us to explain your presence—so many of you. You will need to learn our ways," he said, "and quickly. . . ." His voice trailed off.

"Learn your ways?" wailed Richelle.

"Wait a minute," Jeremy said. "Just wait a minute. We ought to think. Have you got any change in your pockets, Quinn?"

Quinn shook his head.

"Well, I do have these little-bitty earrings," Richelle volunteered, "and they have gold posts, I think. I could leave them, I suppose." She lifted her hair away from one ear to show the possibility.

Good old Richelle and her many trips to the mall, thought Jeremy. It was something, at least. But the old woman shook her head. "It is not enough," she whispered. "Only something very dear to you can be counted as something of value in this exchange."

Real despair washed over Jeremy. He felt dizzy and sick. He held tight to Austin and let himself slump against Quinn. Maybe Quinn would think of something.

"Get off of me," Quinn said under his breath. "This thing is digging a hole under my arm already."

"Quinn!" Jeremy stared at him, and Quinn stared back, and in a moment they nearly knocked over the little bench in their haste to get up. "I almost forgot! Quinn *does* have something of value," Jeremy crowed. "Really!"

"It's true," Quinn said, his voice breaking with excitement. "At least I think I do! It's the most important thing I own, or sort of own, anyway." He unzipped his jacket. "Do you think it's all right to leave it here?" he whispered to Jeremy. "Do you think my dad will ever speak to me again?"

Jeremy rolled his eyes. "Do you need a brain transplant, or what?" he whispered in return. "Listen, Quinn, the only chance you have of getting back to your dad at all is to leave that thing here. It's the only chance for any of us. We have to try it, don't we?"

"Right!" Quinn said, swallowing hard. "Stand close to me, Jeremy." With his jacket open, he unbuckled the belt he wore around his chest and laid it, scabbard, dagger, and all, in the wizard's lap.

"Oh, Quinn!" Richelle caught her breath when she saw what it was.

"Wow!" Austin said, inching closer. "Cool!"

The wizard himself seemed surprised. He bent his white head quickly over the weapon, pulling it out of its sheath and holding it down toward the fire, where the polished blade gleamed in the light. Harket ran his finger lightly along one keen edge and then the other. He studied the pattern of inlay on the handle, then held it out for Berta to see.

Jeremy fidgeted. "Is it something of value?" he asked at last. "I mean, enough to get us home?"

"Perhaps," murmured Berta, making Jeremy worry that she did not seem sure. "You will have to try it and see," she said.

The wizard nodded slowly. "In our world, the thing itself has great worth," he said, holding the boys with a sharp look. "But I cannot guess what value it has for you in your time. Those who hold as much magic as your people do should have no need of things that cut and kill."

"Well . . ." Quinn said, and could go no further.

"It's old," Jeremy said. "We haven't ever really used it ourselves." It didn't feel like the right explanation, but it was the best he could do.

Harket studied them all a moment longer. Then he snapped his fingers once, and Duchess went to him and stood quiet. With one slice of Quinn's dagger, the wizard freed her from the leather strap that had made her a captive.

"Children, you must go," he said.

"Hurry," Berta told them. "The wind is freshening, and dark is coming, and it will be cold this night—"

"We're going," Jeremy said. "Believe me, we're going." But when Richelle took Austin's hand and moved toward the door with Quinn, Berta held Jeremy back. For a moment he was afraid that he was going to be part of the bargain himself. But the old woman only pulled up his sleeve and in one swift motion covered his forgotten wound with ointment. He opened his mouth to protest until he realized how good it felt, and then he kept quiet.

The wizard's wife put her mouth to his ear. "By the morrow, you will not have a mark," she whispered.

Thank goodness, Jeremy thought. His mother would be sure to ask questions.

"You will not need a scar to remind you," Berta said. "For the others, the traveling will fade and seem like a dream, and soon be gone. But you will not forget. They who shed their blood in our land, hold us fast in memory."

Jeremy began to feel as if he couldn't breathe. "Okay," he said. "Sure. Thanks, Mrs. Harket. Thanks to you both." He saw the dog following Quinn out the door, and he tried to hurry after them, but Berta caught his sleeve again.

"Listen well, boy," said the wizard's wife. "If the gift of the dagger takes you only as far as the edge, the rest will be up to you."

"What do you mean?" Jeremy looked from Berta to Harket. "What do I have to do?"

"Do not try to plan it out, boy," the wizard said. "You will know what to do when the time comes." He rose and laid one hand for just an instant on Jeremy's head. If there were such things as tiny lightning bolts, Jeremy thought, they would feel just like the wizard's fingers.

"Now go," Harket said. "The others will be waiting."

The old woman stepped to the door and pushed it wide for him. Jeremy managed to raise one hand in a gesture of good-bye, and then he ran.

Duchess had already taken the lead in the gloomy light, and the group struggled up and around and through, as before, taking turns helping Austin. Jeremy tried to keep his feelings in check, tried not to worry about what might happen at the edge of the ravine. But his heart beat fast as they neared the top. He didn't care how much trouble they were going to be in, if only they could get home. Just below the crest they all stopped and drew together, and Jeremy gave Duchess a pat. She thrust out her nose and sampled the air ahead.

Richelle began to chant softly. "Please, please, please."

Quinn took Austin's hand and stepped ahead. "Come on, Austin. I'll help you up," he said, sounding just the way Quinn was supposed to sound.

"Let me come with you!" Richelle said, hurrying after her brother as fast as she was able.

Breathing hard, Jeremy buried one hand in the long hair on Duchess's neck and stayed tight to her side as she climbed a little way off to the left of the others.

"Everything okay over there?" he called. With Duchess, he was about to take the last step up out of the twilight of the ravine, and he was filled with foreboding. What if it didn't work? Then one of the dog's paws went out of sight, over the top, and Jeremy felt like cheering. If Duchess could get out of the ravine, they could surely all get out. He let go of his hold on her. He didn't want to hurt her when he scrambled over the edge.

"Hey, are you guys okay or not?" he called again.

"I don't know!" Quinn shouted. "It's too slippery or something over here. We keep sliding back."

Jeremy's foot was braced against a stone that began at that very moment to wobble. He grabbed a branch and clung to it as his foothold fell away, and then he could do no more than just hang on. None of his muscles seemed able to pull him any closer to the top. He was too flustered now to answer even when Austin called to him. He struggled to remember just exactly what Berta and the wizard had said. The rest is up to me, he thought in desperation. But what did that mean?

Duchess waited for a while, and then she went on, pulling herself up and over. When she reached the top, she turned to look back down the bank at him, her pale eyes agleam in the fading light, her ears twitching. "Where are you, girl?" Jeremy whispered. "Are you home?" Duchess looked different to him, somehow. She was the same beautiful dog all right, but she had a new air of watchfulness, of restlessness. Maybe she really was a little like a wolf, he thought, or maybe she was just waiting, although he didn't know for what.

Something moved then in Jeremy's mind, the shadow of an idea he didn't want to have. "Oh, no!" he said to himself, his face buried against the arm that held so tightly to the branch. "That can't be it!" But he knew all at once, and with absolute certainty, the thing that he had to do. It was the only way that he and Austin and Quinn and Richelle could all go home. Even now he could hear Austin crying. Jeremy scrubbed his free hand across his own eyes and cleared his throat so his voice could be strong.

"Duchess," he said, "you're the best dog ever, and I thought I could keep you until I was old, like nineteen or something. But now"—he stopped to swallow—"now you need to go wherever you belong."

The dog cocked one ear, shook herself, and stepped down over the bank to Jeremy as smooth as running water. She paused beside him to lick the hand he held out to her. "Good-bye," he whispered, and then she was gone, disappearing silent as a wild thing into the ravine.

For a moment Jeremy was too numb to move. Then he kicked at the bank, found his footing on a new stone, and scrambled upward. He drew in a great breath of new air. "Quinn!" he shouted. "Quinn, try it again!"

"Hey!" he heard Quinn say. "It's okay now! We're up! Wow, it's darker up here!"

And it was. Jeremy blinked and let his eyes adjust. Finally he saw lights, and they were the lights glowing from Mrs. Ramey's windows. And then in an instant there was Mrs. Ramey herself, waving a flashlight in their faces and crying out to the neighborhood: "Here they are, everyone! Here they are! I've found them!"

❖ Ulf

They had sent him with his captain to stand watch far up the riverbank that first night, when the princes' half-loaded vessels still lay at anchor in the water. The soldier soon found a place to sleep, and so Ulf huddled as good as alone while other warriors gathered back at the washing stone to raise their cups to victory, and sing and shout until they too slept. He fidgeted under the weight of the cloak someone had given him, and the new cuff chafed his wrist. His mind raced ahead of the river to the sea beyond and the unknown land of Zirn that would be home to him. The journey that had filled him with such anticipation by daylight was losing some of its appeal in the dark. An old loneliness settled over him. The wind was cold on his face, and he thought fondly of his nights in the wizard's hut, of the warmth and the chanting and the pungent smoke.

In the midst of this remembering, Ulf saw a shadow moving toward him, cutting through the night's thin ribbons of mist. He understood it was his duty to run, to raise an alarm for his captain, but his legs and feet had turned to stone. The shadow became a man with white hair and a white beard that seemed to glow as he came soundlessly through the brush.

"Harket?" whispered Ulf. "Is that you?" It was surely an enchantment, the boy thought, else the wizard could not have moved so nimbly.

"I come to bid you good-bye, boy," Harket said, beckoning him.

Ulf was filled with pleasure, and he was surprised that he could stand so close to the wizard without trembling.

"I bring you gifts in parting," said the old man, "three in number, according to custom. First, from Berta, food for your journey." From a carrier under his cloak he produced a packet, which Ulf accepted gratefully. The boy had not been big enough to claim his own fair share when the evening food was passed, and he hid this supply deep inside his tunic.

"Next," the wizard said, "here is something from your traveler friends, something they had to leave behind them."

Ulf leaned even closer, catching his breath. "They are gone now? And the dog, too?"

Harket smiled. "All is well," he said.

Ulf nodded. He felt relief, but sadness, too. And then he saw what it was that Harket was holding out to him. "A dagger!" he cried, seeing the gleam of the blade as the wizard pulled it from its scabbard and turned it side to side. "Do you mean I am to have a weapon of my own?" He could scarcely believe it, even as Harket wrapped the belt twice around his middle, reaching inside Ulf's heavy wrap and under his tunic to make the fastening secure. Pride swelled his chest as he touched the handle and felt the intricate pattern of precious metal and wood. It would have to stay hidden for now, but later, in Gudrun's service, having a weapon would mean much to him, as much as life, perhaps. And this one—this one was grand enough to earn him notice.

"This last is also from your traveler friends," said the wizard, "from the boy Jeremy." The old man whistled low and soft.

It could not be, Ulf thought. He dared not hope. Still, his heart ceased to beat as he waited. And then she came, his golden dog, his heart's desire, ghostlike in the first light of the moon.

"Magic!" he whispered, unbelieving. She came to lie at his feet as if offering him her loyalty, panting with her tongue out, a real, flesh-and-blood dog.

Ulf fell on her neck to stroke and praise her. "Oh, thank you!" he cried softly to the night sky, hoping the other boy, wherever he was, would know his gratitude somehow.

"Thank you, Harket!" he cried to the wizard, and without thinking, he rose to his feet and threw his arms around the old man, embracing him.

"Fare you well, boy," the wizard said. "We will think of you, Berta and I." Then suddenly he was gone, and Ulf was left to stand watch, secretly armed and no longer alone.

"Good dog," he said softly. "Good dog." He was very happy.

❖ *Jeremy*

Jeremy slept snug in his own bed clear through Sunday morning, brunch and all. He was slow getting up, and his head was confused. He was still on the stairs when he heard Austin's voice, fretting softly. Then his mother's words floated up to him, distinct and clear: "Don't worry, Austin. She'll come home. Duchess has run away before, but she always comes back."

Sleep and dreams left Jeremy's mind in an instant. Not this time, he thought, and it was such a heavy thing to know it made him stop right where he was. Things would never be quite the same without Duchess.

And yet Jeremy couldn't help thinking how lucky they all were. They were home, weren't they? They were safe. And although he and Quinn were grounded, at least it wasn't forever. They were going to have a lot of unpaid yard work to do for Mr. DaSilva, too, but even that could have been worse.

Actually, he was a little bit proud of the story he had managed to tell last night, piecing it together as he went, sparing their parents the parts of the truth they wouldn't have believed. It was a good thing for all of them, he supposed, that Austin had fallen asleep on their father's shoulder about one minute after they came up out of the ravine. Later, the things he said about walking like a dog on a leash just sounded like nightmares. And Richelle had done them the favor of falling apart the minute she knew they were safe. By the time she could talk sense again, she was already vague about everything except chasing Duchess and Austin and hurting her ankle and finding the boys in the dark. She kept looking to Quinn and Jeremy for answers to their parents' questions, and Quinn—the first to forget—had left everything about their day in the ravine for Jeremy to explain.

Yet Quinn had confessed to Mr. DaSilva how he had taken the knife from the souvenir chest on a whim, to dress for playing ancient warriors on the hillside. Jeremy had described his part in leaving it there, and they both said they were sorry and wanted to return it, and that's why they had gone back where they weren't supposed to be, and they had lost track of the time. All true, Jeremy thought with some satisfaction. But then Quinn's father had asked why they hadn't brought Quinn's dagger home with them. Couldn't they find it? Would they be able to go back with him in daylight and show him where it was?

Jeremy almost smiled, remembering, for he had been the one to think of an answer.

"Well," he had said to Quinn's father and all the adults gathered to listen, "you know that old prowler guy? We ran into him when we were coming home, and he made us give him the knife, and he kept it." Almost true, Jeremy thought. Really true, in a way. But after he had said it, everyone started to talk about how wonderful it was that they had escaped the ravine unharmed instead of how terrible it had been for them to go there in the first place. That was nice, Jeremy thought. It was just the way he felt himself. If only Duchess could have come home with them.

Later, after Jeremy had cheered himself up with a plateful of leftovers, he spent the afternoon doing the two things he had promised himself he would do. First, he gathered up all his military models—warriors and skirmishers, archers and horsemen, sentries, catapults, wagons, extra weapons, everything. Then he sealed them in a big cardboard box with lots of sticky tape and carried them to the attic while his little brother napped on the family-room couch.

"Are you sure you're ready to put all that stuff away?" his mother asked.

"Uh-huh."

"Saving it for Austin?"

"Maybe. I don't know."

"Austin certainly likes them," she said.

"Yeah, Mom, but what if they're a bad influence, or"—
he paused for longer than he meant to—"or something?"

His mother raised one eyebrow. "Sounds like being in
big trouble has made you think. Is that it, Jeremy?"

He nodded. "And then I wondered," he said, "would it
be all right if I read the story you're working on? The
princess one?" That was his second goal for the day.

She smiled. "Sure. Just finished it this morning, and I'm
so glad."

Me, too, thought Jeremy. Me, too.

He found the folder in her study and brought it back to
the couch where Austin slept. He turned the pages slowly,
almost hearing Ulf's voice. There was Gudrun, refusing to
marry Prince Armut, and the queen who made her do
laundry, and then her brother the prince, and her real
boyfriend the prince, and all the warriors coming out of
their boats. As he came near the end, he took care to read
every word, and he wished he were allowed to call Quinn,
just once. The king and queen were slaughtered, all right,
but Gudrun had stepped in and spared the lives of Armut
and his sister, Orrun. After the journey north and
Gudrun's marriage to Erik and a lot of feasting, Prince Ar
was sent back to rule over what was left of his people. And

then Ar promised to give his sister Orrun to be the bride of Gudrun's brother the prince, just to keep the peace between their two lands. Jeremy put the pages back in their folder with a giant sigh.

"What's the matter?" his mother asked him.

He thought for a moment, trying to figure out how to say it. "I guess I was sort of hoping for a wizard," he began. "A wizard who lives in a ravine not far from the queen's castle, and a boy who goes with Gudrun to be her servant in her new place and everything."

His mother shook her head. "Jeremy," she said, "sometimes I wonder if you have more than your share of imagination." She picked up her coffee cup and started toward the kitchen.

"And I thought there might be a dog, too," Jeremy called after her. "You know, one that looks a little bit like a wolf."

Austin sat straight up, his nap over. "What dog?" he said. "Where? Is it Duchess? Is she home?"

Jeremy ruffled the little boy's hair. "Not yet, pal," he said. "And maybe she won't ever come back, you know, because sometimes dogs get lost for good and someone else finds them and gives them a good home."

Austin began to sniffle, and Jeremy thought fast. "Probably, if Duchess doesn't come home, we'll get another dog. At least I think so."

"A puppy?" Austin's voice was hopeful.

"Well, yeah." Jeremy thought about it. "Sure. It would have to be a puppy, I think." His own voice took a hopeful turn. Maybe by the time he and Quinn weren't grounded anymore, there would be a puppy to keep them all company, to take the place of those ancient warriors he wasn't going to touch, ever again. He smiled.

"Hey, Jeremy," said Austin, "where do you think Duchess is right now, this very minute?"

Jeremy shrugged. "Don't know," he said. "But I could tell you a story about her."

"Do it!" said Austin, snuggling back down on the couch.

Jeremy closed his eyes. He could see the old ravine with the mountain above it, and the wizard's hut, and Harket staring into the fire, and ragged Ulf, who was so brave and kind. "Once," he whispered, "once, a long time ago, there was a boy who was lonely and wanted a dog. . . ."

AUTHOR'S NOTE

The part of this story that takes place in Ulf's world was inspired by a tale called "Gudrun" in the book *German Hero-sagas and Folk-tales*, retold by Barbara Leonie Picard (Oxford University Press, 1958). While I haven't tried to be true to all the elements of the original, as Jeremy's mother would have done, I have borrowed many things and adapted others. If some of those things seem cruel, it may be worth remembering that Gudrun's story comes from a time when values and ideas were far different from those that are favored today.